HIS FIERY HOYDEN

A REGENCY NOVELLA

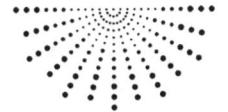

ROSIE CHAPEL

His Fiery Hoyden
A Regency Novella

Rosie Chapel

First printing 2018
ISBN: 978-06482797-4-7 (e-book)
ISBN: 978-0-6450738-0-5 (paperback)

Ulfire Pty. Ltd.
P.O. Box 1481
South Perth
WA 6951
Australia

www.rosiechapel.com

Cover Images Courtesy: Deposit Photos (Image by liqwer20.gmail.com) and Pixabay (Image by Skeeze)
Cover Design: Lisa Miller with Got You Covered

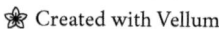 Created with Vellum

This book is dedicated, with much love, to Melanie!
The strongest person I know!

His Fiery Hoyden

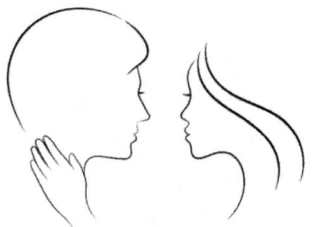

CHAPTER ONE

An imposing carriage rumbled up rutted tracks towards a rather weary-looking cottage. Above the red-tiled roof, plainly in need of repair — numerous holes and cracks patched with birds' nests — smoke curled lazily into an azure sky from one of three squat chimneys. The expanse of austere grey stone was interrupted by a smattering of spotlessly clean windows, in turn, softened by brightly coloured curtains flapping in the breeze.

The carriage, emblazoned with a coat of arms, came to a halt. Four enormous black horses, their bridles gleaming in the sunshine, stamped restlessly until a command from the driver, who jumped down to drop the step, settled them. A man, attired in smart livery, climbed out and, a trifle disdainfully it must be admitted, studied the house for several minutes before walking down the flagged path to the front door.

Rapping the iron knocker, he stood patiently, a slight smile tugging at his lips at the sounds of laughter coming from within. The door was flung open, and a small tow-haired boy of indeterminate age stared up at him.

"Good afternoon, sir. May I help you?" The lad enquired politely, his green eyes alight with curiosity.

The man bowed. "Good afternoon to you too, young man, am I speaking to the head of the house perchance?"

The lad chortled with laughter. "Livvy! There's a gentleman here thinks I'm the head of the house." He slapped his knee and bent double with mirth, his childish glee wresting a responding chuckle from the uniformed man. A flurry of footsteps and a petite young woman came to the doorway, placing her hand on the boy's shoulder

"Now then Sasha, no need to be cheeky," she scolded gently, her smile removing the sting from her admonishment. She turned her gaze to the man, who was arrested by her dark grey eyes, eyes which belied her apparent age. "I do apologise for my brother. I think perhaps he forgot to collect his manners when he collected the eggs this morning."

"It is of no matter Miss…" he paused delicately, but it appeared the young woman saw no necessity to apprise this stranger of any personal details yet, so he swallowed and continued, "…I have herewith a letter regarding the Duke of Albermarle's grandson, Alexander Harrington." He handed over an official-looking scroll. Not folded, this was rolled and tied with red ribbon.

Livvy undid the knot and unfurled the creamy vellum, noting the Albermarle seal at the bottom, her fingers smoothing over the richness of the paper as she flattened it. She started to read, but the words seemed to bounce around, not helped by the fact the paper kept rolling back into its tight coil.

"I cannot read this out here, I need something to hold down the corners. Please, sir, do come inside for a moment. I am sure you would appreciate a cup of tea and perhaps a slice of cake. I baked it this morning."

Instructing the child to take the driver a drink and some

sugar biscuits, as well as apples for the horses, she smiled her invitation. The caller found himself sitting in an aged leather chair near the fire, in a cosy room, before he realised what was happening. Livvy — he presumed she was the 'Livvy' to whom the boy referred — bustled about in the adjacent kitchen, returning with a pot of tea and a plate on which stood a huge cake, lemon sponge if the smell was anything to go by. His mouth started watering.

Placing a large slice on a fine china plate, Livvy passed the cake, along with a good strong cup of tea, to her visitor before moving to a table tucked under the window. Unrolling the document, she laid a heavy book on the top of the sheet to prevent it springing back on itself and, holding the other end in nervous fingers, began to read.

She read it through several times, trying to get her head around the contents, her mind in a whirl. Livvy had long since presumed no one in the Harrington family knew or cared where Sasha and she were. This was the first instance, in her recall, anyone had bothered to make contact. The sole time she had felt brave enough to write to the duke was when Tristram and Elinor Harrington, Sasha's parents, were ill with fever.

She had sent two letters. One informing the duke of his son's illness, the second of his death. Neither missive had engendered even the briefest acknowledgment, so she made no further attempt. She wanted nothing from them, but Sasha was the duke's grandson, a grandson he had never even met.

In Livvy's limited experience, people tended to be grief-stricken when a family member passed away, and Sasha's father had been the only son of the Duke of Albermarle. She could not comprehend how Tristram's death and that of his wife, at so young an age, failed to warrant any kind of response from his father.

Regrettably, none was forthcoming. Livvy had tried to carry on with her life, left to bring up her baby brother with no help, no income and no one to care whether they even survived the next winter. The last six years had been difficult, and Livvy was not about to let some self-important member of the *ton* dictate either to her or Sasha. He was all she had.

She took a deep breath to calm an old anger. It was not this man's fault; he was the messenger, not the instigator.

"Mr…" She raised a quizzical eyebrow.

"Edwards," he supplied.

"Mr Edwards, thank you for delivering this letter today. I fear your journey has been in vain. Please inform your master, Sasha is happy here with me and there is more chance of hell freezing over than of my brother dancing attendance on his Grace." Her tones were saccharine sweet, but Mr Edwards did not miss the glint in her eyes — which had darkened to the hue of a storm swept sky — or the tension in her jaw.

"Miss Livvy," he appealed, "please reconsider. His lordship wants what's best for young Alexander. He'll want for nothing. Would you deny him that?"

He could see his words struck a chord, but as he watched, a mask dropped over Livvy's face, and she straightened her back.

"While I am sure that is true, the duke ought to have considered these things six years ago when I informed him of the death of his only son. We have managed thus far without the trappings of wealth, and I believe myself an adequate teacher." Lifting her chin, Livvy dared her guest to contradict. "I understand all the arguments about inheritance and tradition, but until I can be certain Sasha will be cared

4

for in a manner to which he is already accustomed, I cannot in all conscience release him into the duke's guardianship."

She drew another, rather tremulous, breath. "I know we live a spartan existence, Mr Edwards, and doubtless the comforts of Harrington Hall would be most convivial. That said, all the luxuries in the world cannot outweigh a gentle hand when you need guidance, a warm hug when unwell and unconditional love, which I believe I offer Sasha right here in my unassuming cottage. I accept I cannot keep him from his inheritance forever, but I feel it is preferable to let him make up his own mind when he is of an age to consider all his options."

She blinked fiercely and looked down, brushing non-existent fluff from her apron, while she attempted to stem a sudden rush of tears at the thought of losing Sasha. Gaining control, she raised her head.

"Thank you for taking the time to deliver this letter. I am truly sorry your visit was wasted."

Accepting this for the polite dismissal it was, Mr Edwards took his leave, surprising Livvy by bowing over her hand, before climbing into the carriage. The driver clicked the reins, and the four beautiful horses clip-clopped back along the dusty lane.

Mr Edwards ruminated over her words. He was a little puzzled by some of them, but it was not his place to question either his master's directive or the woman's response. Never-theless, her slightly barbed remarks had left him feeling uncomfortable, and he hoped Lord Cranfield would be sympathetic to her concerns.

❧

Livvy tidied the parlour, covering the cake, and washing the crockery, stacking everything to dry, while mulling over the conversation. Needing to expend some nervous energy, she called Sasha, asking whether he fancied taking a walk with her into the local village, to help her carry the supplies she needed. With no income, Livvy had to rely on her skills as a needlewoman, and the copious batches of eggs their chickens lay, to barter for any food they could not produce themselves.

❧

Without making a fuss, the villagers did what they could to support Livvy and Sasha. Piles of chopped wood would mysteriously appear at the cottage gate in late autumn, a block of cheese, or slab of butter — neatly wrapped in paper — would turn up on her doorstep.

A thick blanket or a winter cloak, in fact, any items of clothing their previous owners had grown out of, but still with plenty of wear left in them, were gathered together, cleaned, folded into a basket, and delivered when Livvy wasn't around.

The young woman was very grateful and made sure she left home-baked tasty treats at the back of the church for her anonymous benefactors.

❧

The afternoon was almost over by the time they arrived home, tired from a long day, but with everything Livvy needed. Sasha had plied her with questions about their visitor, and she had answered as best as she was able. Once she discovered the truth of Sasha's ancestry, Livvy had spent hours with the local vicar, gleaning all she could about dukes and titles and primogeniture. She had begun explaining the convoluted issue to the child as soon as she deemed him old enough to understand.

Unsure of the Harrington family's feelings on the matter, she divulged what she knew without colouring his perception. Thus, while Sasha was aware of the laws of inheritance, he was more interested in chasing the calf around the paddock than learning to be a duke.

By the time they had eaten dinner and Livvy had read him a story, Sasha had all but forgotten the man and the shiny carriage and the four proud horses.

Livvy, unfortunately, could not forget, and the gnawing worry her life was about to be tipped on its head, yet again, gave her a troubled night.

CHAPTER TWO

The next morning, Livvy was woken by a loud banging. Groaning, she turned over and squinted out of the window. The sun was barely brushing the horizon, so it was very early. Who the dickens needed her at this time of day? Calling that she would be there in a moment, she indulged in a quick wash in the basin next to her bed, brushed her teeth and plucked a clean dress from her wardrobe.

Slinging an old, but warm, wrap around her shoulders, she raked her fingers through her curly hair, twisting it into a fairly respectable bun, while she ran down the stairs.

The banging began again.

"I'm coming, I'm coming!" She shouted, yanking open the door to scowl balefully at the extremely tall and extremely well-dressed stranger propped against the frame. "Who on earth are you, and whatever is the meaning of such rude behaviour at an hour even the birds refuse to acknowledge?" She demanded, her sleepless night leaving her churlish.

"I have come from Harrington Hall to collect the Duke of Albermarle's grandson."

Livvy frowned. "And I told his messenger yesterday, the duke's grandson won't be going anywhere until he's old enough to make an informed choice," she retorted, her lip curling at the almost insolent expression of the man in front of her. "Be off with you and tell his highness that since it's taken him six years to register Sasha's existence, it might well be another six years before we bother to acknowledge his."

She tried to slam the door but failed to notice the visitor's polished boot in the way, and it bounced back, catching her in the face.

"Son of a b..." she swallowed on the expletive, her cheek smarting from the impact.

"Hell, I didn't expect that to happen. Are you all right?"

"I'll be fine," she mumbled through her hand, which was cradling her aching jaw. "Please go."

"No! I cannot return to Harrington Hall without Alexander. 'Tis more than my life's worth," he countered, shoving the door wider and moving her hand to inspect her face. The blow had been a hard one, causing Livvy to bite the inside of her cheek. Blood coated her lips, and a bruise was beginning to bloom on her pale skin.

"The devil, you *are* hurt. You need to make sure it's clean. It was my fault, let me help?"

The entreaty sounded genuine, but Livvy stumbled backwards, trying to get out of his way. His bulk filled the doorway, and he towered over her in the narrow hall.

"Sir, do not trouble yourself. Go and tell the duke to mind his own business and maybe, just maybe when Sasha is older, he might decide to pay court." Retreating to the parlour, Livvy sounded as though her tongue had swollen, her words indistinct.

The man frowned as he tried to work out what she was saying. "Stop being so fractious, here..." he took her arm, and plonked her down onto the closest chair, "...now sit there like a good girl and let me help."

He went into the kitchen, opening cupboards. Finding a bowl, he filled it with water, before adding a good pinch of salt from the pot on the bench, making Livvy's eyes widen; his knowledge at odds with his persona. In truth, her face was aching badly, and she was fighting an unexpected urge to cry. It was so long since anyone had cared for her well-being, and it made her feel vulnerable.

He opened drawers until he found a suitable cloth, then came back and, moving the other chair alongside Livvy's, sat down. He placed the bowl on the table and dipped a corner of the cloth into the salt solution.

Squeezing out the excess moisture, he dabbed at her lips, cleaning the blood, rinsed it in the sink and repeated the action until all the blood was wiped away.

Before pouring the water out, he instructed Livvy to swill some around her mouth making sure she let it wash over the bite mark, as often as possible. He got her to do this a few times, and by the time he was satisfied, Livvy felt quite peculiar. Her head was thumping, and her cheek was throbbing.

All this and she didn't even know his name.

While the man cleaned the bowl and rinsed the cloth out yet again, Livvy leant her aching head against the back of the chair, listening to his random chatter. He had a rather nice voice — deep and almost musical — she could listen to him talk all day. Her mind wandered, and before she knew it, she had fallen asleep.

Philip Harrington — or to give him his official title, the Marquis of Cranfield — coming back through from the kitchen, studied the sleeping girl. Small of stature, she was thin, almost gaunt, and her face was too pale. Dark hair, an odd shade — somewhere between chestnut and black — curled around her head coming loose from the bun, into which she had so desperately tried to tame it before she opened the door.

In his opinion, not at all pretty. His thoughts strayed to a certain, classically beautiful lady who would be arriving at Harrington Hall in the not too distant future.

He ran his eye over her one more time, sprawled in the chair, arms folded across her stomach. She was a feisty one and no mistake. He hadn't known what to expect after Edwards' return the previous day. Her 'hell freezing over' comment had tickled him, and he decided he might try to persuade her to see reason. The implication he had ignored Sasha for years sat badly with him. He only found out a week ago the boy existed.

There was obviously more going on here than he was aware. This girl for one. She called Sasha her brother yet as far as Philip had been able to ascertain, his cousin had one child not two. Who was she really, and how did she fit into this sorry little tale? While observing her, his sharp ear caught the sound of footsteps coming down the stairs.

A tousled head appeared, and then wide green eyes peeped around the door, followed by a mouth in a perfect 'O.'

"Who…?" He broke off when Philip put his finger to his lips and pointed at Livvy.

"Who are you?" The question a fierce whisper as the boy came right into the room, his nightshirt half tucked into his breeches.

"I assume you are Master Alexander Harrington." The

boy nodded warily. "I am your cousin, Philip," came the quiet response.

Sasha stood, his head cocked to one side, his thumb creeping up to his mouth. A childish habit he still reverted to when nervous.

"Shall I make you breakfast?" Philip asked.

Sasha shook his head. "No, sir, no eggs yet. Livvy usually collects them while I get dressed."

"Would you like to show me where the hens are, and we'll collect them together? Then I can make you something to eat while Livvy sleeps."

"Why is she sleeping in the chair?" Sasha tiptoed over and looked at Livvy, noticing the angry bruise on her cheek. "Did you hit her?" His whisper became infuriated, and he ran at Philip, fists pumping.

Philip bit down on a chuckle, easily avoiding the onslaught, swinging the boy into his arms and, carrying him out of the back door into the cool of the early morning, stood him on the flagstones.

"No, I did not hit her. She tried to slam the door, but my foot was in the way, and it bounced back, smacking her hard in her face, causing that bruise. She'll no doubt be sore for a couple of days but no lasting damage."

Sasha glowered at him suspiciously, prompting Philip to contemplate whether the two were related after all. Both seemed equally truculent.

"Come, let us go find those eggs, then maybe you and I could have a chat."

Sasha dithered for a moment then decided if Livvy had let this man into the house he couldn't be too sinister and led Philip along neat pathways to the hen houses at the bottom of the garden.

"We need to milk Bessie too." Sasha slipped his small hand trustingly into Philip's larger one, tugging him towards the doe-eyed cow in the field next to the garden. A little wicket in the low hedge swung open at Sasha's touch, Bessie and her little calf strolling over to inspect the newcomer.

'This is Claude,' Sasha said, waiting for Philip to get on with the business of milking while he stroked the calf who stood quietly next to his mother.

"I'm afraid I cannot milk a cow, Sasha. I don't know how," admitted Philip, apologetically.

Sasha glanced at him in surprise "Really?" He quizzed. Philip nodded. "Goodness, I thought everyone knew how to milk cows. Wait a minute…" Sasha ran back to the house, returning seconds later, swinging a pail, a damp cloth slung over his shoulder. As he came through the gate, he unhooked a stool from under the roof of a low wooden lean-to and dropped it next to Bessie.

Squatting on the stool, Sasha showed Philip how capable he was. First, he used the cloth to clean the cow's udder, before carefully squeezing the teats to clear the milk ducts. Then he stood the pail between his knees to hold it steady, his head resting against Bessie's bulk.

Firmly, but gently, Sasha repeated the squeezing motion, warm milk soon spurting into the bucket. He kept at it until the pail was about half full then, making sure the lid was on securely, carried it with both hands through the gate and set it on the path.

Then he took Philip's hand once more and led him to the hen house. The smell of warm straw and fowl assaulted Philip's nostrils, and he was hard pushed not to sneeze. How did people live with these kinds of smells all the time?

"It's a bit strong, isn't it?" Sasha said sympathetically, patting his cousin's hand. "I'll wager you wouldn't even notice it after a day or so." His bright eyes and cheeky smile eliciting a responding grin from Philip.

"I am not convinced, but I will take your word for it, young man. Now, where are these eggs?"

Sasha shooed the hens outside, before showing him where the perfectly shaped eggs lay in nesting boxes arranged along both sides of the hen house. He collected all of them in the straw-lined bucket suited for the purpose, then gingerly passed it over for Philip to carry.

"I might drop them," he said, conspiratorially. "Livvy always worries about that. We can't break any, we barter some of them you see." Leaving Philip to speculate how these two actually survived, if they had to barter with eggs. Shaking his head, he followed Sasha back into the kitchen — collecting the milk on the way.

Seeing Livvy was still asleep, Philip draped a soft blanket, he found on one of the other chairs, over her. She murmured something but didn't wake, snuggling into the warmth of the blanket, falling deeper into slumber.

"She was worried yesterday." Philip raised an eyebrow at Sasha's comment. "A man came to take me away, and she doesn't want me to go. I don't think she can manage without me." Sasha confided.

"I think you are probably right," assented Philip. "Now let me see whether I can whip up some breakfast for us both."

Diverted, Sasha showed this man whom he'd known less than an hour, where Livvy kept the cooking implements, and how to light the stove.

The two enjoyed a very enlightening conversation while they tucked into poached eggs and toast, the contents of which, for some reason neither mentioned to Livvy.

CHAPTER THREE

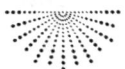

*L*ivvy stirred. She had been basking in a wonderful dream. One which resembled the folk tales she liked to read. Something about a handsome prince and the damsel he saved from a monster. As she awoke, Livvy became aware her body felt stiff, and she couldn't work out why.

Opening her eyes, she realised it was because she was not in her comfortable bed but in a chair in the parlour. She shot up. The muscles in her legs protested and crumpled under her and she barely stopped herself from landing with an unladylike thump on the floor. *Some damsel.*

Grabbing the arms of the chair, she hoisted herself up, glancing around in confusion, vaguely recalling talking to a very tall man, and banging her cheek. Her face throbbed dully. She ran her tongue around her mouth, feeling the lump where she'd bitten the inside of her cheek — that part was correct then. What about the man? Where was he?

Voices wafted in through the open back door, and she walked slowly through to see two heads close together chattering away like magpies. Her heart thudded while she observed them, for although one was much younger, their facial features mirrored each other. Even their hair was almost the same colour.

There was no doubt the stranger was related to Sasha. She was going to lose her brother and, even accepting this was the best thing for him, Livvy could not prevent the acute wave of loneliness washing over her, nor the resulting whimper.

The two on the step did not miss the soft sound, both turning at the same time, their quizzical expressions identical. Unable to stop the tear from trickling down her cheek, Livvy spun around, busying herself at the sink.

She sensed movement behind her. Two small hands clasped her waist.

"Livvy, Livvy! This is Philip. He's my cousin. I've never had a cousin before. He helped me milk Bessie and cooked breakfast..." Sasha gabbled on about what they'd been doing while she slept.

Livvy turned and met Philip's green eyes, so like Sasha's, over the top of her brother's head. He smiled tentatively, but she couldn't respond in kind, there was nothing to smile about. She drew her anger at the Harrington family over her like armour and stared mutinously at this man who was about to tear her life apart.

"I wonder whether you might spare me a few moments?" Philip asked, when Sasha finally took a breath. "I have a proposition which I believe will work out well for all of us."

Keenly aware she couldn't prevent Philip from taking Sasha, Livvy really had no alternative but to listen. She wasn't going to let him know that though, holding his gaze for what seemed an interminable moment before inclining her head ever so slightly.

"Sasha, sweetheart, please go and get dressed and put your nightshirt in the basket. Those breeches too, there's a clean pair on your chair." Sasha nodded and skipped up the stairs singing a tuneless ditty, his voice fading the higher he climbed. A loud bang, then silence.

"Please, take a seat." Livvy ushered Philip to the two big chairs fanned out around the hearth. "I am sorry, I haven't yet had time to light the fire."

Philip waved aside her apology, intrigued by her refined manner and cultured tones. She didn't speak with a local accent. This piqued his curiosity, at the same time as he acknowledged now was not the time to question it.

"The morning is warm." He waited until they had made themselves comfortable. Leaning back, he rubbed his chin in a rather absent gesture, while he gathered his thoughts.

Livvy said nothing. She sat rigidly upright. Her expression reminiscent of a prisoner awaiting the final judgement.

Philip's heart did an odd lurch. He ignored the sensation and set out his proposal.

"Before I go into detail about my plan, there is something of which you need to be informed. Until a week ago, I had no knowledge of your existence, of the existence of either of you. I admit I was stunned when I discovered I had a cousin but understood him to be in the care of his parents, not someone scarcely more than a child herself."

Livvy bristled at the implication she was not fit to care for Sasha. Philip didn't give her any time to counter his words, continuing,

"Then yesterday Edwards informs me, Alexander's parents died from fever six years ago and that my cousin — the heir to the dukedom — is living in a hovel with some young woman claiming to be his sister."

Livvy leapt out of the chair, glaring daggers at him. "How *dare* you call our home a hovel? How *dare* you come in here with your fine clothes and your expensive education and your... your fine clothes, implying I am not family to Sasha, and incapable of caring for him? Where was all this interest six years ago when I wrote to the duke of his son's illness and death? Where was all this concern when I had to struggle to get food on the table, wood to keep us warm, and clothes to wear?

"I was not even ten and four when they died and Sasha still a babe. We had nobody but each other, and I fought to give us a life we could be proud of. I planted vegetables, took in mending, eventually able to barter for hens and a cow. I learnt how to cook and clean and care for a baby as well as the animals now reliant on me for their lives. Have you *any* idea how hard that is? Of course, you haven't! I doubt you have ever had to lift a finger in your pampered life unless you chose to do so. You sanctimonious fatwit!"

Livvy's voice rose to a shriek, her hair swirling around her head almost crackling with the force of her wrath. Her distress, palpable.

She was not yet twenty, she had lost most of her childhood. She had lost two sets of parents, and she was about to lose the most important person in her life. Livvy glowered at Philip for long moments her chest heaving. As quickly as it flared her outrage faded, leaving nothing in its wake. Nothing at all.

She drew a steadying breath.

"How could you be so heartless?" Her voice had no inflection, her face was devoid of expression, and her eyes had gone from grey fire to empty slate. "If you intend to take Sasha, I will not stand in your way, but I cannot witness his departure. I don't suppose you care to take his clothes, but I beg you, don't let him forget his books, oh and his bunny. I know he might be considered too old for babyish toys," she hastened to explain, "but he cannot sleep without it, and it does no harm. Please tell him goodbye. Mayhap I will see him again one day."

She turned and fled the house, running down the path into Bessie's field and out onto the moors, the tears, which had been threatening since the previous afternoon, pouring down her cheeks. In her heart of hearts, she knew this day was inevitable, and that to be with the Harrington family was the best thing for Sasha.

He deserved so much more than she could ever hope to offer but it didn't mean she was ready; she didn't know whether she would ever be ready. Perhaps it was better this way, the decision no longer hers, but she couldn't watch him leave, she just couldn't.

꧁

Philip was frozen in place by her tirade.

"Dammit, that was not how it was supposed to go," he muttered. He had a plan, he thought it a fine plan, but he hadn't had the chance to outline it. His throwaway comment about this ramshackle building sparking her blistering burst of temper. He couldn't understand her reaction at all. Surely the chance of living at Harrington Hall was better than living here?

While this ran through Philip's mind, his gaze took in the clean surfaces, the handmade blankets and cushions, the cheerful window furnishings. The parlour was neat and tidy, yet cosy. A set of shelves laden with books filled one wall. A few old, yet sturdy and comfortable-looking chairs were scattered around the room, and a huge basket, all manner of material spilling out, was tucked against the table by the window.

Intrigued, and despite knowing he was prying, Philip spent a few moments exploring some more of the house. Yes, it was in desperate need of new furniture and floor coverings, but every room was as snug and as spotless as the one before. This house was loved.

He recalled what Livvy had said about looking after Sasha. This firebrand of a girl, woman, had devoted the last six years of her life to raising his cousin. How old did she say she was when her parents died? Not even ten and four... that meant she was probably barely ten and nine now. Hell's teeth, at ten and four he had been at Eton, spending school holidays at his family's London home, or at one of their country estates. He had never wanted for anything — ever. Clothes, food, warmth, comfort, and luxury, these things he took for granted, and Livvy's scathing comments made him stop and think.

He needed to revise his plan.

Sometime later, when Livvy still hadn't returned, and Philip was starting to feel uneasy, Sasha reappeared, looking perturbed. He was clutching a tattered toy, more patches than original material — this must be the bunny Livvy had mentioned.

"Where's Livvy?" Sasha's thumb was already in his mouth, and his eyes were like saucers.

"We had a disagreement, and she's gone for a walk to cool down."

"Why?" he whispered.

"Things might need to change, and Livvy is finding the notion rather... errr... challenging."

Sasha sidled up to where Philip was standing and, once more, slipped his hand into that of his cousin. "What might change?"

Philip looked down at the child and decided to tell him everything. Sitting in the chair and lifting Sasha onto his knee, Philip explained his plan. He was careful not to denigrate anything Livvy had worked for but highlighted the advantages of living in more salubrious surroundings.

"W-what about Livvy? I d-don't want h-her to be on h-her own. Sh-she doesn't l-like being on her own." Panic setting in at the thought of leaving behind the one person who had always been there for him.

"I was hoping we might persuade her to come with us for a time until you settle in, and then we'll see. Do you think she might like that?"

Sasha pondered this. After a little while, he nodded. "I think so, it would nice for her not to work so hard all the time," he said, seriously.

Philip hugged his young cousin. "Now that's decided, where does your sister like to walk? I think it's high time we went to find her. We have a lot to do."

"There's a track at the far side of Bessie's field, leading across the moor. Livvy often goes that way, it's wild and lonely, and she says it makes her insides smile. I don't know what that means, but if she's happy, I'm happy." Sasha shrugged, clearly mystified by Livvy's odd turn of phrase.

Philip felt a grin tug at his lips as the two of them made their way out of the house, through the garden and onto the moors.

CHAPTER FOUR

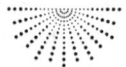

*I*t didn't take them long to find her, sitting on the bank of a stream, lost in thought. Birds zipped about collecting nesting material — some thinking Livvy's riotous curls, lifting in the breeze, might prove quite satisfactory. Livvy didn't seem to notice. Her legs were pulled up, one arm looped around them, chin pillowed on her knees, while absently tugging at the mossy grass with her other hand.

Philip paused, unwilling to have her steely eyes accuse him again, to hear that dead tone in her voice. He wanted her to smile, but for why eluded him.

Sasha ran across the springy ground and flung his arms round Livvy's neck. "Livvy, Livvy, don't be sad. You can come with us, you can come and have fun at Hamming... Hallingt... where Philip lives," he said, giving up on the title of the Albermarle estate.

Livvy got hold of Sasha's hands and swung him around onto her lap. He snuggled against her, and held him close, pillowing her cheek on his silky hair. "Have you been talking with your Cousin Philip?" she asked quietly, as a long shadow fell across her.

Philip sat on the grass next to them. He studied her tear-stained face, reading the upset and confusion in her eyes. "Please accept my apologies, Livvy. The last thing I intended was to hurt you or question your care of Sasha. You must see, to be in the home, which is his birthright, to learn how to become a duke is as important as feeding chickens and milking cows."

He held her gaze, gratified, after a tense moment, to see a small nod. "What I wanted to ask before my mouth ran away with itself, was whether you might agree to accompany Sasha, to spend as long as is necessary with him to make sure he is happy."

"Then what?"

"What do you mean?"

"What happens once he's happy and settled, and becoming who he was born to be? Will you send him off to school? To Eton or Harrow, one of those far away establishments for sons of the elite. And what about me? Will I have to be all prim and proper while a guest in your home? Will I be expected to engage in ladylike pursuits? For I warn you, that is not something I would ever agree to. What about my, our, home? Who will tend to it while I am swanning around a mansion? Cows don't milk themselves you know, and despite my best efforts, my chickens cannot be trained to open a sack of feed."

Livvy sighed. "My life is here where 'tis hard work, but simple. I am not versed in the ways of the *ton* and have no desire to prostrate myself in front of those who consider themselves better than me. Here, I am safe where no one is trying to mock me or humiliate me for being who I am."

Sasha interrupted, "Please come Livvy, Cousin Philip will get someone to help here, I'm sure."

The guileless faith her brother had in his cousin's ability to fix everything like magic, amused Livvy, and she hugged him tight, dropping a kiss on his scruffy head. "Thank you, darling, let me think about it. Perhaps your cousin and I need to discuss it in more detail but, if you would like to go with him today, I have no objections."

Philip held his breath; this was an unexpected about-turn. He shot Livvy a glance, but her expression was no longer readable, her face closed. He could not imagine the thoughts running through her head, nor did he especially want to. It was doubtful he featured positively in any of them.

The little boy played with his fingers, twisting them around and around, his face screwed up in concentration. Moments ticked by with agonising slowness, or so it felt to the two waiting for his answer.

"We...ll," Sasha drew out the word, "if you think you can manage without me, I would like to see Cousin Philip's home..."

Livvy made an odd sound.

Sasha put a finger on her lips "...I will go *if* you promise to come too, as soon as possible."

Livvy felt more tears building and didn't trust herself to reply straight away. She had no intention of looking like a milksop in front of this tall, grave man who exuded power and control. Burying her face in Sasha's hair, she took a deep breath, then another, then another until she felt able to speak without her voice wobbling.

Forcing a bright smile, Livvy tucked a finger under his chin, lifting his head so she could look him in the eyes. "Sasha, my brave and strong protector. 'Tis a hard decision, but one I think, you will not regret. Cousin Philip and your grandfather will look after you. They will teach you the ways of the nobility, but do not forget what it is like to be without all the trappings of luxury, for that will make you a most sympathetic and respectful duke when comes your time."

She hugged him again, then pushed him off her knee, before uncurling her legs and standing up. "Right, shall we go and see what you might like to take with you."

Philip was keenly aware she had made no promises at all.

She held out her hand. Sasha gripped it tightly, offering his other hand to Philip, who, swallowing his delight at Sasha's decision, hauled himself off the grass and took hold. The three set off back to the cottage, the boy chattering away garrulously about his upcoming adventure, not noticing in his excitement, that Livvy didn't say a word.

§

Shortly thereafter, when Sasha had been persuaded not to take the whole of his bedchamber with him, that the Hall would have a bed and blankets and pillows and a wardrobe and a box for any toys, the two cousins were ready.

While Sasha was supposed to be sorting out what to take, the two adults discussed the possibility of Livvy accompanying them, unable to come to a decision with which both were happy. Livvy was not prepared to leave the cottage unattended. She had vested too much in making it productive and wasn't about to let all her hard work go to waste.

She was under no illusion how this would turn out. Sasha would likely forget her soon enough, no — maybe not forget — but she would become someone he saw occasionally. His new life would take precedent, and that was as it should be. He was, after all, the grandson of a duke, it was his inheritance.

Livvy believed it would be easier without her presence; he worried about her too much.

Sasha was not yet eight years old, too young to be

concerned about his older sister. He should be playing, learning to ride, being a child. Her life would continue exactly the way it had always done, just without him.

Philip wanted Livvy to agree to follow them, but he could see persuading her would take time. She refused even to discuss the possibility of travelling to Harrington Hall, stating Sasha would settle more quickly if she wasn't there.

All they reached was a stalemate.

Too soon, Sasha was ready and, as his rather pathetic pile of luggage was strapped to the back of the coach, he hugged Livvy as though he would never let go.

Livvy's heart ached, the pain was almost unbearable, but she smiled sweetly and held Sasha close, whispering, "I love you, Sasha, never forget that. I am very proud of you, more than you will ever know." Kissing him on his cheek, then again on his hair, she placed his cap securely on his head and stood him away from her, checking to make sure he looked as tidy as possible.

He was wearing his Sunday best — 'best' being a relative term — but he did look smart, and she had managed to drag a brush through his hair. His face was clean, and his boots polished until you could see your reflection in them. He might not be as finely attired as a duke's grandson ought to be, but he didn't look too shabby at all.

"I'll see you soon," she promised, pushing him towards the carriage.

Turning to Philip, she said. "Please look after him. He's a child, and he's never slept away from home before. Here…" she shoved a scrap of paper into his hand, "…these are the things you need to know about him. If I ever hear even the slightest rumour he is unhappy, I will make your life a living hell." She pinned him with her gaze until he inclined his head in acknowledgement. "Now go, before I make a complete ninny of myself. I do not want Sasha to see me cry."

"Please reconsider and come with us, Livvy. I do believe you will enjoy a sojourn at the Hall."

Livvy shook her head. "I cannot leave this," she swung her arm about her. "Bessie, Claude, and my chickens would die, please do not ask me again. I may visit, once Sasha has had the chance to find his feet." Knowing she had no intention of doing so. As hard as this was, she believed a clean break was better for both of them. Sasha had a new life to begin, and he didn't need to cling to the old one.

Philip wasn't done. He had a new scheme churning in his head, but he needed a couple of days to make sure it would work. Then, she would have no alternative but to agree to his terms. So, all he said was, "I will take the greatest care of Sasha and keep you updated on everything he does. Thank you for being so understanding. I accept this situation is less than desirable and please believe me when I say our door will be open to you, always, should you change your mind."

He bowed over her hand and then, for no reason he could think of, brushed a kiss to her fingers. He felt them tremble, at the same time as he was visited by the most peculiar sensation that her hand nestled into his as though meant to do so. Shaking it off, he walked to the carriage, climbed in, picked up the reins and clicked the horses.

Sasha leant over the back, yelling goodbye, and waving madly, making Livvy think he would fall out if he wasn't careful, a relieved smile curving her lips when she noticed Philip's arm snake around him, holding him steady. She waved until they were out of sight and all around her fell silent.

Bereft, she walked slowly back into the house. A house which seemed eerily still and utterly empty. Unsure what to do, Livvy trailed upstairs to Sasha's bedchamber to tidy it up. She straightened the bed covers, folded the clothes strewn all over the floor, dropped his remaining toys into the basket where he kept them, and stacked the few books he had left, neatly on the shelf.

Livvy stood for a while, looking out of the tiny window, the view from which she would never tire, the day's events tumbling through her mind. Yesterday, everything was normal, nothing to suggest the tumult about to happen. She was on her own — again. Sasha's departure bringing back bitter memories of the last time she was alone.

❧

When she was not much more than Sasha's age, Livvy had been left to fend for herself in the backstreets of a town, not many miles from where she currently stood, with no memory how she came to be there. She had a vague recollection of her mother, and of her father there was nothing.

Nobody knew what had happened or how long she had been on her own, and Livvy was too young to understand. It was only when she fainted from hunger while begging for scraps of food at the market that a benevolent soul had stepped in and taken care of everything.

Somehow, and Livvy never discovered how, they found a friend of her mother's. Elinor Harrington, and her husband Tristram, immediately took the girl in, treating Livvy as though she was their own daughter. They brought her to this cottage, giving her a comfortable life, and Livvy had loved them in return.

Even when they had Sasha, nothing changed. Livvy became his adoring older sister and willing slave, a role she had continued at the unexpected death of their parents before Sasha was two years old.

She had no idea they were nobility until she came across a letter when both were bedridden with fever. The knowledge had come as a shock. Nevertheless, Livvy had done the right thing, sending a letter to the duke explaining what had happened, but she never heard back.

Sinking down onto the little bed, holding an old shirt to her nose, and inhaling the scent of the child she considered her brother — Livvy let the tears fall.

CHAPTER FIVE

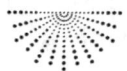

*S*everal miles away, a carriage drew up outside an imposing, three-storey Palladian-style mansion. Warm Yorkshire stone, mellow in the afternoon light, the sun sparkling off rows of mullioned windows, and the crown of chimneys scattered across the roof, seemed to welcome its new owner. Sasha's eyes were wide, Harrington Hall was enormous. Never in his life had he seen anything so big.

"Do you live here?" he squeaked, his jaw hanging open as several uniformed men rushed out to help the passengers down, carry the suitcases, and lead the horses to the stables. Sasha was speechless when the men bowed to him... *to him*. It was somewhat overwhelming, and he wished Livvy was with him. She never panicked and always knew the right thing to say.

"I think, maybe I should go home," he muttered, shifting awkwardly from foot to foot.

Philip smiled in understanding. "I know it is a lot to take in, but everyone here is excited to meet you, and soon you'll be right at home."

"What if Livvy needs me? She's never had a night without

me you know." He stared dubiously at the door from which more, smartly dressed, people hurried out. Sasha hid behind Philip hoping they wouldn't notice him. When the group reached them, his cousin gently brought him around to introduce him to those whom, he was about to discover, were his staff.

"Sasha, these are the people who will make sure you have everything you need. What say we show you around?" Philip smiled in encouragement

"Only if you come too," the lad entreated.

"Of course. Where would you like to explore first? Your bedchamber, the stables, the ballroom?"

Sasha gaped at Philip. "What's a ballroom?" he whispered, and just when Philip didn't think the boy's eyes could get any wider — they did.

"A place where people dance, but also good for sliding on your bottom," Philip whispered back, dropping a wink.

"Let's go there first." Sasha grabbed hold of Philip's hand, and the two began to explore.

Once Sasha had gone to bed that night, stupefied by the sheer size of his new home, even his bedchamber was cavernous, Philip went into his study, intent on getting to the bottom of Livvy's accusations. Harrington Hall had been under Philip's care for some time, his uncle preferring London to Yorkshire.

Ignorant of Sasha's existence until the reading of the will following the unexpected death of the old duke a month ago, Philip became wholly responsible for its upkeep until his young cousin was capable of assuming his birthright. It was a role he had gladly undertaken but, evidently, all was not as he had been led to believe.

Philip withdrew a swathe of yellowed papers from his desk. He had found them in his uncle's private office and, prior to this moment, had given them naught but a cursory glance. He untied the string binding the sheets neatly together and began to check each one rather more thoroughly than he had previously. Most were inconsequential missives about estate business or invites to Society functions, but two stood out.

To the Duke of Albermarle,
   Harrington Hall,
   Please my Lord Duke, please, your son and his wife are terribly sick with fever. I do not think I am able to reduce it or care for them properly. If you might send a carriage for them, they could come home to you and be treated by a doctor. They have a child, Sasha, and I fear he may also fall victim to the same illness. I am but one person, with no means of getting them the help they need.
   We live at Rose Cottage, Oak Tree Lane, Redhaven...

Written in a tidy but immature hand, the writer went into detail regarding the symptoms the couple were exhibiting, impressing Philip with her knowledge and eloquence. She concluded with another plea to send a carriage for them. The second one was shorter but no less poignant.

To the Duke of Albermarle
   Your Graceness,

Philip felt a smile twitch his mouth at the childish form of address.

I am sorry to inform you, but both Elinor and Tristram Harrington died during the night. I did write to tell you they were sick but received no reply. Thankfully, your son and his wife were too ill to be told this. Please send a carriage to the address on my last letter so they might be buried with the proper ceremony. Their son, Sasha — Alexander — is here and survived the fever, but he is a babe who has lost his parents and would likely benefit from the care of his grandfather. I beg you to respond for I am at a loss as to what to do.

Yours faithfully
Miss Olivia de Courcy

Philip read both letters several times. Livvy's despair was clear in her words. He had not realised Sasha was struck down by the same illness. *How did Livvy manage?* He tapped the letter against his chin, pondering over what she had done when she heard nothing from the duke. More than this, where had Tristram and Elinor been buried, and who had helped her?

This alleged neglect jarred with what Philip recalled of his uncle, who had never been anything other than loving and kind. His behaviour completely at odds with the cold-hearted image this letter evoked. A wave of anger shot through Philip, almost robbing him of his breath. *He had to set this right.* Somehow, some way he had to do something to compensate for such callous indifference.

On the plus side, he now knew Livvy's full name — which sounded vaguely familiar, although he couldn't recall from where — and thus, would be able to instigate enquiries into her background. Sliding the two letters back into the pile, Philip tucked the whole lot into his drawer, which as an afterthought, he locked.

A week since his arrival and, although slowly adjusting to his new home, Sasha continued to miss Livvy, often waking in the night crying out for her. Philip — a new plan in place — decided a day out in the country might prove restorative. Early one morning as the sun was beginning the long climb to its zenith, they set out. It wasn't long before Sasha realised where they were headed, jumping up and down on his seat in glee.

The horses had barely come to a standstill when Sasha hopped down, running up the path calling for Livvy. At a quiet word, the driver and an estate worker, whose presence was key to the success of Philip's plan, remained with the coach. Philip strolled after the lad in a far more sedate fashion.

Stepping through the open door, he was met by silence, then Sasha's high-pitched tones floated in from the garden, words tumbling over each other in his haste to tell Livvy about his time at Harrington Hall. Philip followed the sound, through the cottage and out into the sun-drenched garden.

Even with his limited knowledge, it was apparent to Philip, the large assortment of vegetables was thriving. Livvy obviously tended her crops diligently. He could see her, at the far end near the chicken coop, leaning on the fence listening to Sasha's uninhibited chatter.

He walked towards them, spotting Livvy's bare feet and the ragged tear in her skirts. He had no mind to comment, instead saying, "Miss de Courcy, is it not glorious? We thought it an excellent opportunity for a drive through the countryside."

Wondering how he had discovered her surname, Livvy flicked him a suspicious glance, conscious she was not dressed to receive callers. "Good morning, my lord." She sketched a curtsy, rubbing grubby hands on a small piece of cloth tucked into her apron. "Might I enquire as to the nature of your visit?" Her tones not overly encouraging.

"I have a proposition to put to you." He bent and whispered something to Sasha, who grinned, nodded and shot off, through the house banging doors as he went, yelling what sounded like 'Bernard.'

"Who's Bernard?" Livvy quizzed, bewildered.

"He's one of my gardeners, and he is going to tend to your home and your land while you come back to Harrington Hall with us for a few days. Now before you get defensive..." when Livvy started to shake her head, "...Sasha hasn't been sleeping properly. He often wakes in the night calling for you, and he frets about what you have to do now he's not able to help. He is worried you cannot manage without him. I think he would settle better if you were close by. Bernard is eminently capable of looking after your property and all that comes with it."

Despite her head telling her this was a ploy to guilt her into accompanying them back to the Hall, Livvy listened intently while Philip outlined his plan. Although he went into great detail, basically, his suggestion was, she return with them and see whether her presence alleviated Sasha's little anxieties.

Once satisfied her brother no longer needed her, she could either stay or return to the cottage to carry on with her life. He couched it in far more persuasive terms and perhaps allowed her to believe Sasha was more upset than he really was, but that was the general gist.

"Do you think that is a scheme with which you might be agreeable?" Philip asked when he thought he had talked for long enough.

Livvy dithered. She certainly didn't want Sasha to be moping, neither did she want to interfere with his new life, but all of a sudden, the thought of spending a few days without having to worry about anything at all, was most appealing.

She wasn't about to let Philip think he could win her over quite this easily though. "Let me think about it." She hedged.

Philip nodded. To push her would not give him the answer he wanted.

"Now, might I please meet this Bernard person?" She pushed herself off the fence and headed up the path. Sasha came back through the house chattering gaily to an older man, whose weather-beaten face was wrinkled in amusement as he answered the boy's multitude of questions.

Philip introduced Livvy to Bernard. The two immediately began an animated discussion regarding when particular vegetables are best planted, the benefits of certain herbs, and whether the ivy clinging to the back wall of the cottage should be cut back to root before the autumn or left until after winter.

Philip stood back, observing their interaction, intrigued by Livvy's countenance. No longer the bristling spitfire he had come to expect. Her face was alight with interest and her smile radiant enough to light the whole of his estate. Her hair, which was loose, flowed around her, blood-red highlights glimmering in the chestnut richness.

Philip shook his head. He shouldn't be thinking this way. She was nothing to him, merely someone to whom he owed a debt, yet his eyes kept straying to her mouth as he wondered what it would be like to kiss her.

❧

An hour or so later, after Livvy had pressed a cup of tea and some fresh ginger biscuits on her visitors including the driver, she was propped against the door frame, looking out over her garden, thinking about Philip's proposition. The fresh air, mixed with fragrances of honeysuckle, lavender, rosemary, thyme, and sage, which never failed to lift her spirits, now helped to banish the confusion in her head.

The sun was shining, the sky was blue, and for a moment everything seemed perfect. Why should she give this up, even for a brief period? Then her gaze ran over the shed, which was dilapidated and probably wouldn't last the next winter. The fence needed fixing, and the roof needed new tiles. The money she could make from her mending and the sale of produce would never cover all of this.

A thought popped into her head. She ignored it, but it persisted. Livvy mulled it over, while she listened to Bernard and Sasha, the former's deep rumbling voice in stark contrast with the latter's high-pitched prattle.

Did she dare?

CHAPTER SIX

*P*hilip was standing in the shade of a tree near the garden wall, listening to Sasha explain to Bernard, in serious tones, how to look after Bessie and Claude. He turned on Livvy's approach, his expression hopeful.

Livvy swallowed and, straightening her shoulders, launched into her little speech. "My lord," she began. "I admit to being tempted by your offer and am inclined to agree, howev…" she raised a hand when Philip started to speak, "… might I ask for something in return?"

Philip frowned. Something in return? Surely a visit to Harrington Hall ought to be more than enough recompense. He studied her face seeing a wariness lurking in her eyes and a tension in the way she held her body. She wasn't comfortable. Whatever she was going to ask of him, did not come easily to her. Rather than pay heed to his head and rebuff her, he followed his heart and nodded, waiting.

. . .

"Once my time at your home comes to its natural conclusion, might I be so bold as to request you ask the duke to arrange for my roof, my fence, and my shed to be repaired? I doubt I will be able to raise enough coin to pay for one, never mind them all." She did not lower her eyes as she made her petition, but her humiliation at virtually having to beg for assistance was evidenced by her stance and the hectic colour staining her cheeks.

Philip felt something shift deep inside of him at this young woman's desperation, a desperation she would never admit to. He thought about the six long years she had struggled alone, realising while, to her, the cost of repair would be colossal, to him it was hardly worth mentioning.

"I think that would be the very least the duke could do for you, Livvy and I am more than happy to agree to your terms on his behalf." He reached out his hand, gratified to feel her cold one slip into it as they shook on the deal. Livvy relaxed with a huff, trembling a little from her audacity. "Shall we tell Sasha?"

Diverted, Livvy smiled, and they stepped out into the sunshine.

It didn't take long for Livvy to pack her meagre belongings. She dug out her best gowns, which happened to have been her mother's — well Sasha's mother's — neatly packed away so as not to get damaged. The attire Livvy normally wore was old and well patched. While suitable for someone who spent most of her days in the garden, they were woefully inadequate for somewhere as refined as Harrington Hall, and she was determined not to embarrass either Sasha or Philip.

Taking a last look around her bedroom, Livvy remembered the trinket hidden away inside a handkerchief at the back of her drawer. A simple gold locket, with an inscription on the reverse and a tiny drawing inside, it was the only thing she owned which belonged to her birth mother, and she didn't feel comfortable leaving it behind. Tucking it into her luggage, she started down the narrow staircase, to be met by Philip who, shaking his head in exasperation, took the trunk from her and carried it out to the waiting coach.

Livvy felt confident leaving her smallholding in Bernard's capable hands. She offered him one of the spare bedrooms, which he had accepted gratefully. Even though his family home was not too far away, living in, so to speak, was more convenient. After handing him a list of the shops to which he could sell excess produce, Livvy thanked him for being so kind as to do this for her.

"Tis naught, Miss Livvy. Makes a nice change to have a proper plot to tend, instead of his lordship's flowers." Bernard said placidly, earning a bright beam from Livvy and a quizzical brow from Philip, although the latter didn't appear unduly perturbed by the comment.

Sasha spent the journey to the Harrington estate telling Livvy all about what to expect and, did she know you could actually slide along the floor of the ballroom on your bottom? Listening to his enthusiastic chatter, Livvy realised whatever was going on at night, Sasha was enjoying his new life.

By the time they came to a halt in the expansive court-yard, Livvy knew the names of all the horses, the dogs, the footmen, the grooms, and the kitchen staff, in that order, which amused her no end. Sasha, it seemed, preferred the company of those on the lower steps of the domestic ladder, rather than that of the stewards, the butlers, and the valets.

She was assisted down from the coach by a smartly

dressed footman to whom she curtsied and thanked, causing Philip to grin and the footman to blush.

"You have no need to curtsy to the staff, Livvy," Philip chided, gently.

Livvy felt hot colour wash up her cheeks, her embarrassment mirroring that of the footman. "I'm sorry," she whispered.

"Nothing to fret about, Miss," he replied soberly, a slight roll of his eye and droop of one eyelid making her giggle as he lifted down her small trunk.

"This way, Livvy." Sasha took her hand, dragging her towards the very grand front door.

Livvy was held speechless when she stepped over the threshold. The enormity of the hexagonal entrance hall making her blink in disbelief. It looked larger than her whole cottage. At the centre, a grand staircase led up to the first floor where it split into two lazy curves. One swept around to the second level, the other to the floor above.

From underneath they reminded Livvy of a vast spiral. Their polished wooden banisters gleamed in the sunlight which poured through myriad stained-glass windows to create a glimmering kaleidoscope of colour over every surface.

"Oh, it's like being inside a rainbow." Livvy gasped before she could stop herself, mesmerised by the elegant beauty of the space. A low chuckle reached her ears, and she flushed self-consciously.

"Sorry, I… it's just I've never… well…" she dried up. What could she say?

"Don't apologise, that was the nicest description of this hall I've ever heard. Come, we'll show you up to your bedchamber, where you might like to freshen up after the dusty carriage ride, then we will meet in the library. I'll have Edie fetch you when you're ready."

Livvy followed Philip and Sasha up to the first floor and along a carpeted corridor to a room at the far end.

"This is next door to Sasha," Philip explained. "I thought you might feel more comfortable being close to him."

Livvy smiled in gratitude as Philip opened the door into a charmingly appointed room. She started to back out, shaking her head, stunned. "No, no, I cannot sleep here. This chamber is for royalty, surely? I would be more suited to a room in the domestic quarters."

"Livvy, this is your bedchamber for the duration of your stay. 'Tis one of several guest rooms, and adjacent to Sasha. There is nothing remotely special about it." Philip's no-nonsense tones made her feel like a naughty child, and she marched right into the room to be brought to a standstill once again as she gazed around.

A bed the size of her bedchamber at the cottage was positioned between two sets of glass doors, each of which opened onto a stone balcony. Opposite, a broad hearth in which a fire already burned removing the chill from a room long closed up. An escritoire with its cushioned chair stood alongside the bed and, on the farthest wall, a wardrobe. Livvy wanted to laugh at the incongruity of so large a piece of furniture for her cloak, five dresses, two pairs of shoes, and one pair of house slippers.

"We shall leave you to change. Edie will be along momentarily to assist and then escort you to the library, where there will be hot coffee and something to eat. We might take a stroll around the gardens before dinner, but not much else today, there will be plenty of time to explore."

Livvy, who unusually for her couldn't find her voice, was only able to nod her acknowledgement.

"Don't be long Livvy, there's so much to see." Sasha's treble tones faded as Philip ushered him out, closing the door behind them.

❦

Livvy stood for a long moment, then walked slowly around the room, touching the rich wood, stroking her fingers over the exquisite furnishings and the lavish, yet cosy bed coverings.

Something teased at the back of her mind. A room not dissimilar to this one, although not quite as opulent, a small child being swung in the arms of a dark-haired man, laughter echoing around hallways. Livvy shook her head in confusion. *Where had that come from? Was it a lost memory or just a dream?*

Presuming it to be her rather vivid imagination, she forgot about it, and opened her trunk to lift out her few possessions. As she was hanging up the last of her gowns, there was knock and, at Livvy's invitation, a young girl came into the room, bobbing a curtsy.

"Good afternoon, Miss. I'm Edie, and I'll be your maid."

"Hello Edie, how lovely to meet you. Thank you so much, but as you can see, I have little need of a maid. I'm sure everyone here knows my status is lower than yours."

"Get on with you, Miss, I never heard the like." Edie took over, helping Livvy into a gown of pale lilac, before brushing her hair until it shone, then pulling and twisting it into a simple bun, a few ringlets left to trail over her shoulders.

Livvy didn't own any delicate underclothes, hers were bought or made for warmth not style, but Edie produced linen stays, a cotton chemise and a pair of silk stockings, ignoring Livvy's protest that these were much too fine for her. When the maid had finished, Livvy didn't recognise herself.

"Edie," she breathed. "Oh, goodness me, Edie, you have magic fingers. I look quite presentable."

Edie grinned at Livvy's expression. "You look beautiful, Miss, if you don't mind my saying. Allow me take you to the library." Edie led Livvy along the corridor and back down the magnificent staircase, along yet another corridor to a set of double doors. Knocking quietly, they heard a muffled 'enter' and, opening the door, Edie said: "Go on, Miss, they're over by the fire."

"Thank you, Edie," Livvy whispered, unaccountably nervous. She straightened her shoulders and gripped her hands into fists, then stepped into the room.

Her jaw dropped.

After what she had seen of the Hall so far, Livvy didn't think she could be surprised, this room proved her wrong. It was like nothing she could have imagined in her wildest dreams.

Stretching out, either side of her was a long, oblong-shaped room, its walls covered with bookcases, so many bookcases. Two-thirds of the way up the wall closest to her and running the full length of the room was a sort of narrow platform, or gallery, accessible by two spiral staircases — one at either end.

On the opposite wall, light streamed in through the numerous windows aligned above the bookcases, as well as from two sets of French doors. One set, halfway down the room between the two hearths, opened onto a flagged terrace; the other was at the far end, through which, Livvy could see neatly tended gardens rolling out towards what appeared to be parkland in the distance.

Three large tables, placed at random intervals throughout the room, were littered with books, maps, and papers. To complete the scene, several generously-sized leather chairs circled the two fireplaces — both of which were crackling merrily.

"Oh," was all Livvy could say. One hand fluttered to her

throat, while she gazed in awe at the room; words, for the second time in under an hour, completely and utterly failing her.

"Livvy!" Sasha's piping voice broke into her reverie, bringing her back to earth. She smiled at his excited face, as he seized her hand and towed her over to one the hearths, where Philip was waiting patiently. On a silver tray stood three tall cups, steam coiling out of them, alongside a plate of delicious-looking cakes.

"I do beg your pardon, I didn't mean to be impolite," she said, sitting in the chair Philip indicated. "It's just..." her eyes swivelled back to the books, fingers itching to stroke the spines and read the titles.

"No need to apologise. Do you enjoy reading?"

"Very much," Livvy nodded enthusiastically, "but we have few books, I didn't know so many even existed."

Philip looked at her in astonishment. "This isn't a large collection. Quite small in comparison with most."

Livvy gaped at him; aware this was the height of rudeness but unable to stop herself. "Oh," she said again. Her limited knowledge of the world around her making her feel rather gauche.

Needing to distract her, Philip handed her one of the tall cups.

She sniffed it. "Is this coffee?"

He nodded. Livvy inhaled again, closing her eyes as the rich aroma teased her senses. She sipped it cautiously, this was her very first taste of the brew, but she had heard about it. There was a small teahouse in the village, coffee was served there, but it was a luxury she could not indulge in, far too expensive. She savoured it, letting the dark liquid slide over her tongue and down her throat. It was quite the tastiest beverage she had ever drunk.

"Goodness me, that is heavenly," she murmured, oblivious

of the effect she was having on Philip, who, unexpectedly, decided he would like nothing better than to be the cause of a similar expression on her face. Sasha was jumping up and down in his chair, begging Livvy to hurry up and finish her drink because he simply *had* to show her the gardens and the stables and the orchards and the Great Park.

"I think we might restrict ourselves to one or two of the gardens today, Sasha. No need to rush at things and the afternoon wears on. Tomorrow you may begin to show Livvy around properly."

Livvy smiled at Philip gratefully. In truth she felt rather dazed, and the thought of tramping around the, undoubtedly, extensive, grounds was a trifle daunting.

"How about you show me this garden," waving her hand towards the French doors, "then maybe we could come back here, and I'll read to you? There must be something suitable in here for you if Lord Harrington is agreeable."

As Sasha nodded his enthusiasm, Philip said, "You are welcome to read anything that takes your fancy Livvy, and please, my name is Philip."

Livvy did not think such familiarity was entirely proper but preferred not to argue with him. She swallowed the last of her coffee and placed the cup carefully on the tray. "Lord Alexander, might you escort me around the gardens?" She stood and dropped a deep curtsy to her brother who thought that hilarious. Sasha went off into guffaws, before grabbing her hand and leading her through the French doors at the far end of the room.

Philip watched them walk out onto the terrace and down the steps to the lawns, following more slowly. Livvy intrigued, frustrated, and fascinated him. She was such a puzzle.

Fiercely independent — part hoyden and, oddly, part lady with a healthy dash of minx thrown in. Still, he supposed he could understand it; it must be hard to trust anyone after relying on no one but herself for six years.

CHAPTER SEVEN

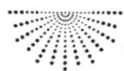

*O*nce back in the sunshine, Livvy started to relax. The lawns were immaculate, trimmed to perfection, and the beds in this garden — as apparently there were several — were full of roses, delineated by neat box hedge, the height of her calves.

Although almost four o'clock, the afternoon was pleasant, long summer days stretching late into the evenings, the light soft and golden. She could hear the drone of pollen-laden bees as they hovered around the blossoms, and the trill of the birds chasing all manner of bugs lifted on eddies of balmy air.

She stood for a moment and let it wash over her, while she admired the spectacular view. The lawns flowed out to a fence in the near distance beyond which was open parkland. She could see herds of deer roaming under the trees and, listening attentively, heard them calling, recognising the bellow of the red and the belching huff of the fallow.

"It's rather nice, isn't it?" Philip spoke in her ear making her jump.

She stepped away. "Yes, it is magnificent. Tell me, how is

it you have red and fallow together? I presumed they would not inhabit the same type of countryside."

Philip raised a surprised eyebrow at her question, taken aback that she would even know the different breeds of deer, never mind their habitat.

Livvy shrugged, deprecatingly. "We had a book on animal husbandry, I needed something to read."

Amused, Philip nevertheless explained. "We have discovered the red are content to roam the perimeter of the park, where it opens onto the moors, whereas the fallow tend to stay closer to the woods circling the edge of the estate."

"How interesting," she said. "I admit to being surprised they would share territory, even on so vast an estate as this. Nature constantly amazes me." Livvy turned and smiled, shyly. "Thank you for this." She didn't elaborate, but Philip inclined his head, in quick understanding.

Offering Livvy his arm — which she accepted, after a brief hesitation — he led her through the gardens, the two falling into easy discussion about the various species of flower and bush they strolled amongst.

Later that evening after a dinner, which had Livvy biting her lip from exclaiming on the — what were, in her opinion — ridiculously large portions, she took Sasha to bed and read him a story out of one the books he had chosen from the library.

"Are you going to stay?" He pleaded. Livvy ruffled his hair and dropped a kiss on his forehead.

"For a little while," she replied, "but you need to be a good boy and go to sleep, none of this waking in the night and disturbing the household. Nearly eight-year-old boys should be able to manage without their older sisters." She winked, and Sasha grinned, snuggling under the crisp sheets, letting Livvy tuck the blanket and quilted coverlet over him.

She found bunny, the threadbare raggedy toy repaired so often it was scarcely recognisable, and slipped it under his fingers, standing for a few moments until she saw his breathing settle into a slower rhythm. Cracking open the heavy curtains to allow a sliver of moonlight to filter into the room so Sasha wasn't disoriented, Livvy blew out the candle and left him to sleep.

Unsure of what she should do, Livvy was heading to her own bedchamber when a shadow loomed up in front of her. She swallowed a squeak when she realised it was Philip.

"Do you always have to sneak up on people?" She scolded in undertones.

"I beg your pardon. I came to ask whether you would like to join me for hot chocolate and maybe a nightcap?" Philip did not look in the least apologetic.

Livvy vacillated for a moment and then nodded her agreement. "That is very generous of you, my lord. I would be glad to join you." She followed him down to the library, which despite its size felt cosy and warm.

After a few moments of silence, Philip asked an innocuous question, and they resumed their comfortable conversation. The evening slid by, and Livvy began to feel quite languid, the result of enjoying two glasses of port — for as with the coffee, this was her first taste of any alcoholic beverage.

"Livvy?"

She blinked hazily at Philip who was leaning forward in his chair.

"Livvy, I found your letters, the ones you wrote to the

duke when my cousin was ill. Might you tell me how you came to be living with the Harringtons?"

Livvy peered at him, trying to remember anything before six minutes ago, never mind six years. Everything was a bit jumbled, and she couldn't be bothered to concentrate. Evidently, her answer was important to him, because he asked her again. Livvy tried to sit up straight, feeling as though she might well be slipping off the chair. Her brow creased, while she fought to recall.

"It was a cold day, and because I hadn't eaten for a while, I was at the market, trying to get some food. My mother…" she couldn't finish that sentence, "…anyway, the next thing I remember was being tucked up in a chair at the back of one of the shops. After that it's a bit blurry," she shrugged, unwilling to revisit so miserable a time.

"Then Mama and Papa came… that's what they asked me to call them." Hoping Philip understood she hadn't presumed. The rest of her pathetic little tale spilled out, somewhat reluctantly, for Livvy had no mind to let anyone feel sorry for her. It appeared the port had loosened her tongue, for she struggled to stem the flow of words.

Philip didn't interrupt or ask questions, letting her talk. When she fell quiet, he found himself staring at her, in awe of her courage.

Livvy shifted awkwardly under his gaze. He was the first person she had unburdened herself to and, although cathartic, she worried he might use her past against her.

Philip could hear her thoughts as clearly as though she said them out loud. "Livvy, please trust me when I say I just want to understand what happened. I promise never to bring it up again unless you wish to discuss it further. I do have one question though." He waited until she inclined her head. "Where are they buried?"

"In the local churchyard. The vicar and the villagers

helped me when…" she took a breath, "after…" she let that hang. "I couldn't move them, and I was concerned for Sasha being in a house with two dead bodies. 'Twas a long time ago, now 'tis just me and… just me." Livvy's barriers came up again, and she wrapped her shawl around her like a shield, drawing Philip's attention to her thin shoulders.

"Have you been sleeping or eating properly since Sasha left?" He dared to pry.

"Of course, I have! What do you take me for? Some weak-kneed ninny, who falls apart at the slightest thing?" Livvy stood, rather unsteadily, scowling at her host. "If you have finished with your interrogation, I think I might find my bed. I expect Sasha will run me ragged on the morrow. Thank you for your hospitality and good night to you, my lord." She dipped an excuse of a curtsy, tossed her head, and marched out of the library, up to her bedchamber.

Philip sat back in his chair, a grim smile tugging at his lips. That Livvy did not like having her well-being questioned was patent, but he continued to worry about her. It hadn't escaped his notice she ate little at dinner, maybe because it was too rich. Doubtless, she was used to plain and simple fare. He would have a chat with Millie, his cook, certain she could provide less extravagant meals. It would probably benefit them all, to eat more wholesome food.

The next few days fell into a pattern. Following an early breakfast, Sasha joined Livvy on her morning walk. A constitutional, the staff called it, to Livvy's amusement. It sounded very grand. After which, the boy would go off for his lessons. Philip had engaged a tutor, who confessed Sasha's breadth of knowledge was prodigious for a child his age. A testament to

Livvy's efforts. He continued to prove himself an apt pupil, soaking up information like dry ground soaks up rain.

During these hours, Livvy disappeared into the library, losing herself in the wonder of all the books therein. Philip usually joined them in the late afternoon, and the three always had dinner together.

Livvy and Philip continued to argue. Both were hot-headed and Philip, who for most of his six and twenty years had been schooled in the ways of the *ton*, seemed to have expectations of Livvy with which she refused to comply. His world was one of rules and conventions, but she was not part of that world — never would be — and, convinced they did not extend to her, chafed against them.

Moreover, it was long since she had answered to anyone. Philip did not own her, nor was she a member of his staff. Despite his generosity in inviting her to stay at Harrington Hall, Livvy believed she owed him nothing more than polite appreciation. Nevertheless, frequent clashes aside, both came to respect the other, and their evening discussions proved stimulating if occasionally heated.

Livvy knew it would not take much to forget her other life. To wallow in the luxury the estate provided, let it seduce her into thinking she belonged in this world. She tried not to become too comfortable, but everyone was so kind and, even though she missed her home, it was lovely not to be constantly worried about where the next meal would come from, or how she would feed the animals. Not that she was about to admit to any of this.

Slightly concerned her brain would atrophy for lack of any challenge, Livvy approached Philip to ask whether she might have a piece of paper to write down her accounts. She needed to be sure, when she returned home, what coin would be necessary for the rest of the year.

Her request was irregular, attending to the accounts was not a typical holiday activity, but Philip had no objection, suggesting the study would be the best place to work. After the third day of doing very little, Livvy ventured into the quiet room and began, painstakingly, to work out what she would require, to see her through the harsh winter months.

As she jotted down the last few details, Livvy found her attention wandering to several hefty, leather-bound ledgers alongside a substantial pile of what appeared to be invoices. Figures fascinated Livvy and, even knowing she had no right, she could not resist the temptation to open them.

Before long, she was absorbed by the income and expenditure of a large estate. Wages for the innumerable staff — *how did one keep abreast of so many people?* she mused — fodder for the animals, cost of ongoing construction and maintenance of fences, carriages, walls, roofs, and estate farms. The list went on and on, it was astonishing.

Without thinking, she started to enter the accounts, double-checking as she went, ensuring she was adding them to the correct ledger.

Philip came into the study. He observed Livvy for a moment, captivated by the way her tongue touched her lip and the absent-minded way she twirled a lock of hair through her fingers, as she worked.

"Livvy?" His curious tone broke into her concentration.

Livvy raised her head and stared for a few moments waiting for the room to come back into focus. When she saw who had spoken, her cheeks reddened and she pushed back from the table, tipping over the chair in her haste to stand up.

Curtsying, she gasped. "Oh, sir, your lordship, sir, I beg your pardon... I was... that is... I'm... well... I like..." she ground to a halt. There was no excuse for her behaviour. She was trespassing in his private accounts and had no business doing so. Righting the chair, she clasped her fingers together and twiddled her thumbs, waiting for the admonishment she deserved.

Philip studied her impassively. Livvy's hair was a mess, unravelling from what he presumed had been a tidy style at some point earlier in the day. Her cheeks were hot with embarrassment and her clothes, crumpled. Not how one would expect a guest in such surrounds to present themselves to their host. Nevertheless, her eyes glowed, something he had not yet witnessed, and caused a thread of something wholly inexplicable to flitter through him, gone before he could grasp it. Shaking it off, Philip came over to the desk.

"Do you like working with figures?" He asked, picking up the ledger and flicking through the pages, glancing at her neat entries and correct additions, surprised by her expertise.

She nodded, unsure of his reaction. "I do, especially accounts. They follow rules and are either right or wrong, which I find both satisfying and soothing," she paused. "I apologise unreservedly, my lord. I had no right, but it was as though I was perhaps helping in some way."

Philip was oddly moved by the fact Livvy felt she should help him. "As it happens, I am not averse. Feel free to work through my accounts to your heart's content."

Livvy breathed a sigh of relief, glad she hadn't caused offence. "Thank you, my lord. I didn't mean to overstep my boundaries. I forgot my place."

"Livvy, your place is here, with us if you could see it. Sasha would love you to stay, and I find your company refreshing. And how many times must I ask you to call me Philip? I have been calling you Livvy since first we met."

Livvy pulled a face. "I'm not sure that would be appropriate, Lord Harrington."

"My name is Philip, and I'm not Lord Harrington, I am Lord Cranfield. If you insist on being so tiresome, I shall have to call you Miss de Courcy…" he let that dangle.

Ignoring this, Livvy dipped a curtsy. "My apologies, Lord Cranfield, thank you for correcting my mistake. Now if you will excuse me, I have something else to which I need to attend." Without waiting for a reply, she brushed past him and was gone before he could say another word.

Amused and perhaps a trifle aggrieved at her stubborn insistence on observing propriety, Philip called for Mr Edwards. He set his steward a task. To find out everything he possibly could about their mysterious Miss Olivia de Courcy.

Conversation at dinner that evening might have been rather stilted if not for the enthusiastic chatter of Sasha, who was learning to ride a pony and regaled them with tales of his misadventures. Too excited at the prospect of riding, he hadn't listened when the groom explained about gripping the flanks of the horse with his knees.

Thus, as soon as the creature moved, Sasha slipped underneath, coming face to nose with his mount who licked him with gusto, before the boy landed with a thump on his backside.

Sasha's embarrassment was exacerbated when the stable hands left him in the dirt, while they chortled with laughter. He was quickly mollified when they hauled him upright, dusted him off, and assured him it happened to everyone the first time, and was soon persuaded back into the saddle.

By the end of the afternoon, he had been able to trot around the courtyard and was looking forward to going out into the Great Park the next day.

"You should come, too, Livvy, I think you would enjoy it."

"Maybe another time, sweetheart," Livvy evaded. "Now it's time for bed, young man. There'll be no horse riding if you don't get a decent night's sleep."

Sasha went with her willingly and was soon lost in dreamland. Livvy did not return to the library, her earlier conversation with Philip playing on her mind.

While Livvy appreciated Philip's request to use his given name, she was concerned it brought her too close. She would be leaving this place soon — out of sight out of mind. Sasha would likely remember her with fondness, but he would be so busy she would soon fade into distant memory.

As for Philip, well, she only ever seemed to vex him anyway, so, she imagined he would be glad to see the back of her. Why the thought of Philip forgetting her should make her feel sad, she could not discern.

A couple of days later, Livvy was once again, buried in accounts, relishing the familiar comfort of numbers. Mr Edwards, prompted by Philip, brought her the latest invoices and, for the past two hours, she had been engrossed in entering them into the appropriate ledgers. One of them caught her attention, tweaking at something in her subconscious.

She read the bill again, rolling the name of the tradesman, the amount and the service provided, around in her head. It came to her like a lightning flash, and she went back through the ledger, finding every entry for this particular tradesman. Each bill was purportedly from a local butcher for a supply of meat. In and of itself this was not unusual. What was unusual was that Livvy knew the local butcher and the name on the invoice was not his.

It was conceivable they were from a supplier further afield, but it niggled her, more especially as the amount was exactly the same on every bill. Surely, the quantity of meat purchased wasn't always the same. One month there might be more pork, another more beef, or fowl. Livvy knew some of the meat was butchered on the estate, which made the accounts even more suspicious. Something didn't add up.

Digging around in one of the drawers, she found some paper and began to make notes. So completely absorbed, she didn't hear the door open, or the sound of footsteps across the floor, nothing until she felt a heavy hand on her shoulder, causing her to jump with fright.

CHAPTER EIGHT

"Who the devil are you, and what are you doing with his lordship's ledgers?" A grating voice demanded.

Livvy glanced up, shaking the hand off her shoulder, to see a thin, rat-faced man leering at her, clearly infuriated. She slid the paper off the desk, folding it into a small square.

"I am Lord Alexander's sister. And you are?" She countered, meeting his gimlet gaze with one of her own.

"I am Mr Stanley, Lord Cranfield's secretary. Now be off, you nosy little madam. This is none of your business." He shooed Livvy out of the chair, but not before she managed to tuck the paper up her sleeve, the contents of the ledger still troubling her.

"My apologies, Mr Stanley," she smiled sweetly. "'Twas just all those numbers looked so pretty." Her tones vacuous, making it sound as though she hadn't a clue.

Mr Stanley looked her up and down, and it was all she could do not to squirm. His speculative gaze verged on lecherous and his eyes lingered rather too long on her décolletage.

Sticking her nose in the air, Livvy breezed haughtily out of the room then, throwing decorum to the winds, fled up the stairs two at a time and along to her bedchamber. Once there, she shut the door, and took a seat at the writing desk, where she smoothed out the paper and re-read her notes several times to be certain she was correct.

One foot tapping on the floor, a nervous habit, Livvy kept coming back to the same conclusion. Someone was falsifying the accounts.

She would have to tell Philip, but how did one broach the subject without it sounding as though she was accusing a staff member of stealing? *Did she dare talk with Mr Edwards?* She knew it couldn't be him, she had seen the steward's writing, and it didn't match any within the ledgers.

She paced the room, wishing she was in her cottage. Nobody could cook the books there. There was a single book and only her. If she messed up, it was her life. Nobody else's was affected. She had gone back scant months, but the amount was, to her mind, astronomical. How had it gone unnoticed?

She recalled the number of ledgers, five she had seen, there might be more. Each one probably dealing with a different aspect of the estate, not to mention the London residence and it was likely there were other houses scattered around the place. She got the impression these dukes had more than one country estate, which sent her thoughts off on a tangent — she had yet to meet the Duke of Albermarle.

Presumably, he wasn't currently at Harrington Hall, for undoubtedly, she would have seen or heard him if so. Maybe he was in London. Shoving that aside, for now, she went back to her notes, after studying them again, decided to have a quiet word with Mr Edwards and Millie, before taking it any further.

With Livvy, to think was to act. She hurried downstairs to

the warm and airy kitchen, inhaling the smell of fresh bread wafting along the passageway. She knocked and walked in.

"Miss Livvy, what can we do for you today?" Millie greeted her through a cloud of flour.

"I wondered whether I might ask you a question regarding the meat?" Livvy ventured, cautiously, hoping Millie wouldn't be affronted.

"Ask away," the cheery cook replied. Livvy explained what was bothering her. Millie listened carefully and being an astute woman understood the problem, immediately. Dusting off her hands, she sat down, pulling up a chair for Livvy.

"So, my sweet, you think someone is skimming coin from his Grace?"

Livvy nodded.

"Wait here a moment," Millie called for Ruby the scullery maid and bade her find Mr Edwards with all haste. Five minutes ticked by with ever-increasing slowness, or so it seemed to Livvy, then she heard heavy footfalls, and the affable steward strode into the kitchen.

"Millie, what is so urgent you had Ruby scurrying like a scared rabbit to fetch me? Ahh, Miss Livvy, good afternoon. How nice to see you," unsurprised to see their guest in the kitchen. "Millie?"

"Tell him what you told me, Miss." Millie waved her hand between Livvy and Mr Edwards, who was, by now, baffled at this unexpected interruption to his day. Livvy repeated her discovery, including the earlier encounter with Mr Stanley, her voice becoming less steady when she noticed Mr Edwards' expression darken.

"I'm sorry, Mr Edwards, sir. I didn't want to speak to Lord Cranfield until I'd checked. I am happy to show you, but I don't know whether the ledgers will still be in the study. Mr Stanley thought I was being overly inquisitive. I let him think I had no idea what I was doing, but the way he looked at me…" she couldn't quite suppress a shudder. Millie caught the steward's eye over Livvy's head, an unspoken message passing between them.

"Don't you fret and leave it with me, Miss Livvy. I will collect the ledgers, and then you can show me what you found. Don't let it worry you today. I'll come and find you tomorrow afternoon while your brother is having his riding lesson." Mr Edwards reassured.

Livvy smiled gratefully and thanked the two staff, relief flooding through her.

Deciding a quick stroll around the gardens would help clear her head, Livvy slipped out through the back door and enjoyed the golden sunlight of the late afternoon. By dinnertime, she had almost put it out of her mind, and the evening passed with its usual ease.

Fortuitously for Livvy and Mr Edwards, Philip had business in York requiring his attention, and he would be away for two days. The next afternoon, once Sasha had gone off to the stables, and when all was quiet, Mr Edwards appeared in the library, where Livvy was engrossed in Troilus and Criseyde, Chaucer's epic poem.

It took the steward several moments to get Livvy's attention, for she was lost in another time. Slowly she became aware someone was speaking, and the real world reformed around her, replacing temples and ancient battles, gods and soothsayers, love and loss.

"Oh, I do beg your pardon, Mr Edwards, I forgot where I was."

The steward grinned and placed the ledgers next to her on the side table. "I have sent Mr Stanley on an urgent errand. He will be gone for at least three hours, now please show me what you found yesterday."

Livvy checked each of the ledgers until she found the one, she had been working on the previous day. Scanning the pages meticulously, her sharp eyes quickly spotted what she was looking for.

"Here," she indicated the most recent one, then showed Mr Edwards the multiple entries, which, at first glance, appeared to be scattered at random through the ledger, but always for the same amount.

"The devil…" Mr Edwards breathed, when he began to see the pattern, "…beg pardon, Miss." The invoices had been shrewdly added to minimise chance of notice. "What on earth made you investigate this further?" He queried, astonished at her acuity.

Livvy shrugged. "I like numbers, and I recognise certain similarities. I wasn't entirely sure. I haven't gone through any of the other ledgers, but I knew there was something questionable about these entries. That an account for a butcher would be exactly the same on every bill, is impossible. Not on an estate as large as this. Besides, I know Fred, the man in the village, and the moniker on the invoice is not his. Neither did I suppose it could be from within the estate, for that would not make any sense."

Mr Edwards, impressed with her grasp of estate business, concurred. "I agree. I think we should go over the other ledgers to ascertain whether the same thing is repeated in any of them, possibly under the guise of a different trade.

"Oh, I hadn't thought of that, sir. Goodness, whoever is behind this is very cunning." Livvy sounded almost in awe at the sheer audacity of the culprit. "Poor Lord Cranfield. I cannot believe someone would steal from him, 'tis unacceptable." Her face contorted into a fierce grimace at the notion.

Mr Edwards laughed. "You do not need to call me sir,

Livvy, and do not fret. Be thankful it is uncovered. Now we can get to the bottom of it. I have my suspicions but need irrefutable evidence before I make any accusations. It would not do to presume and end up implicating the wrong offender."

Livvy nodded her understanding, but one name circled her brain. "You think it is Mr Stanley, don't you?" she posited, very quietly. Mr Edwards held her gaze for long moments then inclined his head ever-so slightly. "He unnerves me," she admitted, which reminded the steward of their conversation the previous afternoon.

Mr Edwards hid his concern well. He did not wish to frighten the young woman; she ought to feel safe here, in his lordship's home.

In the short time since Livvy's arrival at the estate, she had endeared herself to the staff. Always friendly and polite, she often popped into the kitchens to chat with anyone who happened to be there. She had quickly become a favourite of Millie's, the two sharing recipes for all manner of dishes. Mr Warner, the butler, had declared her to be quite the lady, something Livvy giggled at when Edie told her.

Livvy felt at ease behind the baize door and, despite her status being somewhat ambiguous, knew she was not of noble blood with no right to be cosseted by Philip's staff. More importantly, Livvy was a guest, and Mr Edwards had no mind to let anyone ruin her time at Harrington Hall.

"Will you tell the Duke?" Livvy ruminated aloud, snapping the steward from his thoughts.

"He'll not be understanding this kind of thing yet, Miss. He's far more interested in horse riding."

Livvy's brow creased in confusion. "Surely he would want to know one of his staff is swindling him?"

"Eventually, when he's old enough."

"When he's *old* enough?" Livvy expostulated. "He's a father and grandfather surely he's old enough?"

Mr Edwards stared at her in surprise. "Miss Livvy, Master Alexander is the Duke of Albermarle. I thought you knew that."

Thunderstruck, Livvy gaped at the steward, her mouth opening and closing, reminiscent of a stranded trout. The ramifications of the steward's words hit her like a wave crashing on the shore. For a moment there was a roaring in her ears; she gripped the arms of the chair and drew a long, slow, steadying breath.

How had she not known? Why hadn't anyone told her? She ran her mind back over all her conversations with Philip regarding Sasha, realising he had never told her the old duke was dead, nor that Sasha now held the title. Neither had he corrected her assumption he still lived.

She stood up, sat down, then stood up again, and began to walk the length of the room, wringing her hands together. "Why didn't he tell me? All this time, I thought the duke must be in London or at another of his estates. No one told me, and I did not ask, I just presumed. I've been angry with him for so long, and now I find, I have been robbed of the opportunity to vent my ire. How *dare* he leave this world before I could tell him how cruel he was? He abandoned his family. I was there when two of them died, unable to save them..."

Livvy strode up and down, furious mutterings tumbling from her lips. She had never stopped hoping one day she might meet the man who had ignored her pleas. Be afforded the chance to rage at him for his heartless negligence.

"Please excuse me, I need not to be here."

Before Mr Edwards could say a word, Livvy was gone. She rushed out of the French doors, across the terrace, through the gardens and, moments later, vanished into the Great Park.

The steward watched her go, concern written all over his kindly face. He had noticed the interactions between Philip and Livvy and, even though he realised neither had the vaguest inkling what was happening, it was evident their feelings for each other ran deep.

Would one simple omission ruin what the staff dared hope might be possible? Despite Livvy's background, they all believed she was far more suited to his lordship than the lady he was expected to marry, but it was not Mr Edwards' place to advise.

Sighing, he gathered the ledgers and their copious notes, taking them with him to his own office and locking them away securely. He did not want anyone getting a hint of their discovery, deciding to cover their tracks before he had spoken with Lord Cranfield.

❦

Livvy was marching across the parkland, arguing with herself, trying to quash her resentment. She hadn't realised how much she had buried until informed the object of her fury was no longer. Drained, she sank onto a grass hillock, admiring the undulating landscape with its surrounding woodland, the grazing deer, and listened to the twittering of birds.

It was a balmy afternoon, June was sliding slowly into July but, even though she could discern a slight heat shimmer, the day was not overly hot.

Enjoying the sun on her skin and the soft breeze lifting her hair, Livvy was visited by the most unexpected desire to have someone hold her and tell her everything was going to be all right. To assure her, life would get easier. That she wouldn't have to work her fingers to the bone for every scrap of food, or pouch of coin. That her house would stand firm against all weathers and there would be someone to keep her warm at night. Her thoughts spiralled out... *someone to hold her and keep her warm at night*? What was she thinking? Goodness, she was nothing short of wanton.

A face swam over Livvy's vision causing her to suck in a sharp breath.

No, no, this wasn't right, this couldn't be right. He was not destined for one such as her. Unbidden, she recalled their daily spats, his concern the night she had unburdened her past, and his assurance she belonged at the Hall. Livvy growled under her breath as her head finally accepted what her soul had known all along.

The man who irritated and frustrated her, the man whom she seemed constantly to aggravate, the man whose appearance at her door not so very long ago turned her life upside down, had somehow stolen her heart.

Dammit!

CHAPTER NINE

"*Bah!*" She groused to a flock of startled sparrows thinking to land nearby. "Damn and blast it all to h—!" Livvy bit off the expletive. Well, this wasn't good. Thankfully, Philip didn't know, and she would take pains to ensure he never found out.

Doubtless, he was already bound to marry an elegantly refined daughter of a nobleman, and she would return to her quiet little cottage. At least he had promised to ensure it was repaired. She groaned; he had agreed on behalf of the duke. The duke was Sasha. She couldn't in all conscience take money from her brother.

Livvy stretched out her legs in front of her and tried to think of how she might return home without offending Philip. He had been kind enough to invite her to stay at the Hall, he and the staff had made her very welcome. For the first time in her life, she was content; she was sleeping well, her bedchamber was comfortable, and the bed was like sleeping on a cloud. She was also eating more than she ought — this she knew because her clothes were feeling a trifle snug.

It would be a wrench to leave, but there she could not stay, no matter what either Philip or Sasha said. To stand to one side, as Philip married another, whenever that might happen, sent a sharp jab of pain through her chest, making her gasp.

Ruminating over her options, Livvy decided to wait until the end of the week, whereupon she would tell Philip she was homesick and take her leave. Unbidden a tear ran down her cheek at the thought of never seeing him again, but she scrubbed it away and straightened her shoulders. Now was not the time to be a cry baby.

❦

At dusk the following day, the thunder of hooves heralded Philip's return. The Albermarle coach rattled into the court-yard at a fine old pace. Grooms, footmen, and stable boys appeared to tend to coach, horses, rider, and luggage, not necessarily in that order.

Philip, a slender portfolio in his hand, was out of the carriage almost before the step was dropped. He bounded across the courtyard and through the huge doors which were standing open in welcome.

"Warner, my good man." Philip hailed his butler, who was waiting at the door.

Mr Warner bowed. "Welcome home, Lord Cranfield. I trust your trip was fruitful?"

Philip nodded, a broad grin on his face. "It certainly was I am pleased to say." Indicating the portfolio. While in York, Philip spent some of the time researching Miss Olivia de Courcy — Mr Edwards had drawn a blank despite his best efforts. He had unearthed some interesting information regarding his reluctant house guest, the details of which explained why her surname tickled his memory.

Mr Warner advised his master, Livvy was in the library reading to Sasha. Philip hurried along expecting to come upon a peaceful scene. Instead, his approach was halted by the sound of raised voices.

"...rubbish."

Philip recognised his secretary's nasal tones. Rather than burst in, something prompted him to wait.

"What makes you think I have the slightest idea what you're talking about?" Came Livvy's indignant reply.

"Because I caught you snooping in his lordship's ledgers. You think you can pull the wool over my eyes by being sweet and calling the numbers *pretty*? You must think me addled!"

Philip swallowed a bark of laughter at the image of Livvy being 'sweet.'

"Well you shouldn't have been stealing from his lordship then, should you? You slimy toad," retorted Livvy, her voice laden with disgust.

The quarrel became increasingly heated. Disturbed by the noise, Mr Warner appeared.

Philip put his finger to his lips and muttered, "I think we should see where this will lead, Warner. Something is afoot, and I mean to find out what."

Mr Warner joined Philip, the two men listening intently. As neither had any clue as to the reason for such an argument, the recriminations being tossed back and forth were mystifying.

"Why you little bitch! You nosy, good for nothing, interfering busybody. Whatever possessed Lord Cranfield to bring you here is beyond me. You are no better than a cheap strumpet. Maybe that's why. You are only good for a quick toss?"

The enmity in Mr Stanley's voice propelled them forward.

Philip shoved open the door to see Mr Stanley twisting

Livvy's arm with one hand, while his other hovered threateningly close to her throat. Livvy was so angry she seemed oblivious to the man's actions, but it was obvious to Philip, had he not arrived right at that moment, his secretary may well have allowed his wrath to override his sense.

"*Mr Stanley*!" Philip roared, making the two by the fire jump in shock.

Livvy's face, flushed with temper, paled to white, and she clamped her mouth shut. Mr Stanley, unable to contain himself, continued to berate her. His language enough to make the most hardened criminal blush.

"**Enough**!" Philip demanded in stentorian tones, and there was a brief lull. Mr Stanley was breathing hard, his eyes flashing, a malicious sneer curving his thin lips. "What the devil is the meaning of this? Mr Stanley? Livvy?"

Livvy shook her head. *What could she say?* She had no intention of divulging the man's misdeeds. Even though she suspected he was behind the thefts, she had no mind to voice her suspicions in the heat of the moment. She would sound like a snooping gossipmonger. Mr Edwards had assured her, he was going to take care of it. It was not her place to deny him that privilege. Regrettably, Mr Stanley had no such scruples.

"This little guttersnipe dares to suggest I have been stealing from you, my lord. *Me*, who has been nothing but your loyal servant for more than fifteen years! Likely she's the one who is stealing." He sniped in derisive tones. He withdrew something from his pocket, dangling it between them. "What is the bastard daughter of a whore doing with so fine a trinket? Hmmm? Decided to see what you could filch while his lordship was away."

· · ·

71

Livvy gaped at him, her face going from white to bright red in an instant as her fury flared back to life. *It was her locket! How had he found it?* She thought it safely tucked away in a drawer in her bedchamber.

"That's mine," she hissed. "What were you doing in my bedchamber? It was not in plain sight. You have been through my things? And *you* would call *me* a thief?" Livvy launched herself at the secretary, incandescent with rage.

Mr Stanley bunched his fists, his arms lifting in a pugilistic stance. Fortuitously, Mr Warner who had followed Philip into the room was able to grab Mr Stanley before he could thump Livvy, as appeared his intent. Philip hauled Livvy out of harm's way, even as she tried to escape his grasp, bent on retrieving her necklace.

"Give that back, you snivelling little cretin. It's mine, it's always been mine!"

"*This?* Ridiculous! You might have fooled his lordship, but you cannot fool me. How does a penniless slut have something of this quality, unless it was payment for services rendered?" An evil smirk slashed across his mouth.

Cursing her accuser, Livvy went rigid and catapulted herself out of Philip's grip. The latter catching her before she reached the secretary.

"You'll be sorry you ever messed with me." Mr Stanley threw over his shoulder, while the butler strong-armed him towards the door.

"Livvy!" Philip held her against him, tightening his grip when she continued to fight. "Livvy let us deal with it. Mr Warner has Mr Stanley. What is all this about a trinket?"

"It's mine. It was my mother's. I didn't steal it. I've never stolen anything in my life! How *dare* he accuse me of so heinous a crime?" She was trembling, her outrage bubbling.

Philip ushered her over to one of the chairs by the fire, sat her down and draped a blanket around her. He poured a large measure of brandy and told her to sip it slowly.

Livvy, whose teeth were now chattering, took a large gulp, coughing when the spirit hit the back of her throat. By the time she got a hold of herself, Mr Stanley was no longer in the room.

"Now, what in God's name has been happening in my absence? Apparently, I cannot leave the Hall for two days without you causing a fracas."

Livvy pressed her lips together, and a stony silence fell.

"Where is Sasha?" He met her mutinous glare impassively, and after several seconds, she dropped her gaze. "Livvy, please," he gentled his voice, spying the long tremors running through her. "Where is Sasha?"

Livvy raised her head, and he was startled by the anguish in her eyes.

"He's in his bedchamber I believe, or maybe in the kitchens. Millie was making biscuits, and he loves to sit and chat with them, I think it reminds him of ho—" she bit off the last word. It sounded ungrateful. Neither was Livvy sure how Philip would react to that snippet of information, unconscious of the fact he already knew, and had no mind to prevent the lad from mixing with the staff. It gave Sasha an insight into how hard they worked to maintain such an extensive estate.

"Please get my locket back," she entreated, her voice dropped to a whisper. Philip never expected to see Livvy looking so vulnerable.

"Of course. While we wait for Mr Warner to return, would you be so kind as to tell me what that was about?"

"I'd rather Mr Edwards told you. 'Tis his right."

Her voice had no strength and Philip was beginning to

worry. This wasn't like his Livvy. Wait — *his Livvy* — where had that come from? There was another whom he considered to be *his*. Lady Elise Sherrard, daughter of an earl. The lady with whom he attended banquets and balls when in London. The lady who was due to visit a few days hence. She was the one everyone expected him to marry. Livvy was just, well, Livvy.

Even with what he had uncovered, Philip didn't expect that to change. Observing Livvy while she sipped the amber liquid, her thin fingers clenched around the crystal tumbler, he feared it already had.

Despite all sensible arguments to the contrary, Philip was unable to prevent Livvy's waif-like features from appearing at the most inopportune moments. She floated through his dreams, taunting him, whispering his name in far more dulcet tones than he'd heard her employ. She was usually curled up in a chair by a roaring fire in his bedchamber, wearing one of his shirts, which was too big on her, the shoulder slipping down to expose the soft rise of a creamy breast. Long hair falling to her waist in dark rivulets over the white cotton, the flicker from the flames reflecting in her grey eyes.

The previous day he had been in a meeting with a business associate when, unbidden, an image of her lying next to him, her legs entwined around his, sent a shockwave through his body with such intensity, he was forced to remain in his seat rather longer than necessary. This had to stop, it was lust — pure and simple and would surely vanish the moment she berated him again.

Ringing for Mr Edwards, Philip pushed the image aside. Elise was the one he should, he would marry.

Groomed for such a position almost before she could

walk, Elise was wise in the art of being the perfect hostess. An accomplished horsewoman — a necessary skill — Elise was also well-versed in how to manage the social and domestic aspects of an estate, and expert at holding a conversation about nothing at all.

Unflappable, not to mention beautiful, elegant, and refined.

A most suitable wife.

Just utterly boring.

His life would be monitored to ensure he was not troubled by minor inconveniences. Nothing would be allowed to ruffle his day. She would divert all unpleasantness, such things to be dealt with by underlings. If they had children, they would be seen and not heard, much like her attitude to servants. Philip had stayed with the Sherrard's on several occasions and, now he thought about it, he realised the earl's staff never smiled.

His household, on the other hand, was always cheerful. Smiling and joking — friendly but never disrespectful. He recalled how Livvy behaved around them. She treated them the same way she treated everyone. No one was more or less important to her, everyone deserved her consideration, attention, and appreciation. She was open and relaxed with all his staff, from the scullery maid to the gardeners, from the valets to the stablehands, more so than she was with him.

With him, she was either reserved or annoyed, and the realisation cut him to the quick. He wanted her to be comfortable with him. He wanted her to seek him out at every opportunity to share her day, brighten his evening and warm his bed.

Awareness slammed into him.

Oh God, no! How had this happened?

It couldn't be true.

Was he in love with Livvy?

CHAPTER TEN

*A*ghast, Philip took a step away from where Livvy was sitting, needing to put a distance between them. He studied her, huddled in the chair, and fought an unexpected compulsion to hold her in his arms, and kiss her pale face, and tell her she would never want for anything again.

This was going to be tricky. With what he had discovered, Livvy would assume his interest in her was related to her family, her heritage, not because of who she truly was — his fiery hoyden. Then there was the not inconsequential matter of Elise.

He rubbed his hand around the back of his neck. *Blast it all to hell — what a mess.*

Calm reason took over.

No, he wasn't in love with her. This was the result of heightened emotions following the scene he had witnessed, and he was simply worried for Livvy. Of course, a far more logical interpretation for his reaction — nothing more to it. While he was convincing himself, there was a knock at the door and, at Philip's invitation, Mr Edwards came in.

"Lord Cranfield, welcome home. I trust your trip was successful." A respectful bow accompanied his greeting.

Pushing disconcerting thoughts aside, Philip smiled at his steward. "It was, thank you, Edwards. I apologise for the unexpected summons but, on my return this evening, I disturbed a vehement exchange between Mr Stanley and Miss Livvy. Both appeared to be accusing the other of stealing. Mr Stanley was escorted to Warner's rooms where I hope he has calmed down, and Miss Livvy refuses to tell me what's going on assuring me you know all about it."

Mr Edwards glanced at Livvy who shook her head, her normally animated face empty of all expression.

Philip moved away from the fire, motioning his steward to follow until they were out of Livvy's hearing. "Edwards, come on man, spill."

Mr Edwards grimaced. "My lord, Miss Livvy discovered some inconsistencies when she was entering the accounts earlier in the week. She brought them to my attention, and once I grasped what she was talking about, we checked all the ledgers thoroughly. It looks as though someone, and I'm not naming names, has been siphoning money from the estate for some considerable time, possibly years."

The steward explained everything and concluded by affirming that the ledgers were currently under lock and key in his own office. "Miss Livvy didn't think it was her place to tell you. I believe her exact words were, 'his lordship would likely think I'm interfering'. So, I said as I'd tell you on your return."

Philip couldn't prevent a smile at this last, the words so typical of Livvy. "I will deal with it. Thank you, Edwards, and you will be pleased to know my investigation turned up some very interesting information."

The steward raised a quizzical eyebrow.

"I should tell Miss Livvy first, but I am hoping this might convince her to stay here with us."

"Not sure as Lady Elise will approve, my lord." Mr Edwards grinned his delight, unconcerned for the sensibilities of the woman to whom his employer was on the brink of becoming betrothed.

"'Tis not yet her ladyship's decision who lives here, Edwards. Ironically, it is Lord Alexander's," came the considered reply. "That said, I am mindful of how the gossips will view this, so it will involve no small amount of tact." Their conversation was unusual, but Philip had known these people all his life and appreciated that without them, his estate would fall apart. "Please inform Mr Stanley, I will see him promptly at nine in my study."

Mr Edwards nodded and took his leave.

Philip walked over to the fire. Livvy had fallen asleep, nursing the tumbler of brandy, barely a drop left in the bottom. Taking the glass, he stood it on the table. Without disturbing her, he lifted Livvy out of the chair — she weighed little more than Sasha — and carried her to her bedchamber. While he waited for Edie, Philip removed Livvy's slippers, registering how thin they were and once again his heart ached. She didn't even have decent footwear.

Edie knocked quietly and was bidden to enter.

"Please help Miss Livvy into bed, Edie, she has had a bit of a rough evening."

The maid nodded, and Philip left her to it, going next door to find Sasha. His young cousin was sitting by the fire in his bedchamber reading an aged tome of his favourite folk tales.

"Good evening, Sasha," he said stepping into the glow cast by the flames.

"C-cousin Philip. H-how is Livvy? Did that man hurt her?"

"No, Livvy is fine. Do you know what happened, Sasha? Do you feel able to tell me?"

Sasha revealed that Mr Stanley had come in puffed up like a cockerel, yelling at Livvy, calling her horrid names and being rude. Livvy had asked him, Sasha, to run up to his bedchamber saying she would deal with it.

"Maybe I should have stayed, sir. I am the duke after all."

Philip chuckled and ruffled Sasha's hair. "I think your sister did the right thing. Mr Stanley was very upset, and you are too young to handle such disagreeable situations. No harm was done, and your sister managed to foil a thief. Do you, perchance, recall a locket Livvy owns? It's of plain design and looks old."

Sasha nodded. "Yes, it was her... hmmm... I *think* it belonged to her grandmother, but Livvy told me her mother gave it to her. Anyway, yes, it is old, and Livvy keeps it hidden. She said it is the only thing she has from her mother and is special. Why?"

"Mr Stanley accused her of stealing it."

Sasha huffed in annoyance. "No, that is not right at all. She's had it as long as I can remember. Livvy wouldn't steal from anyone, especially you."

"Thank you, Sasha. On a happier note, are you ready for dinner?"

The little boy nodded and slipped his hand into Philip's. The two made their way to the dining room.

"Where's Livvy?" Sasha asked, still unnerved by the recent altercation.

"She's in bed. She was very tired, and I think she needs sleep more than she needs to join us for dinner. Edie will take her something if she wakes and is hungry."

The two chatted through the meal. Philip told Sasha all

about York, the lad begging to go with his cousin the next time he visited. The remainder of the evening passed uneventfully.

§.

Philip endured an acrimonious interview with Mr Stanley. Prior to their meeting, Philip studied the ledgers, Mr Edwards pointed out the discrepancies. As far as they could tell, money had been disappearing on a regular basis for years.

Mr Edwards had found other records written in Mr Stanley's hand, which matched the entries in the ledger. Even though both Philip and his steward were under no illusion that the secretary was the offender, neither was prepared to accuse until absolutely certain.

Despite incontrovertible evidence, Mr Stanley stoutly maintained his innocence. The secretary continued to denigrate Livvy, his comments less than appropriate. He *was* persuaded to relinquish possession of the locket, to Philip's relief.

The interview concluded with Philip indicating he could no longer retain Mr Stanley's services and, although he would not provide references, neither would he take the matter further. Handing his one-time secretary, a bag of coin, Philip suggested he remove himself from the property with dispatch.

Mr Warner and one of the footmen escorted the man to his rooms, waiting until he packed his belongings, then he was taken by carriage to the nearest coaching inn. While most of the staff had no knowledge of the latest upset, Mr Stanley was whole-heartedly disliked, and none were saddened at his departure.

Shortly after lunch, Philip came upon Livvy in the library. She was hunched over the desk, making copious notes, three large books open in front of her.

"Good afternoon, Livvy," he said quietly.

Livvy scrambled off her chair to sketch a quick curtsy, saying, "Good afternoon, my lord." She fidgeted, uncomfortable in his presence now, her emotions too close to the surface.

"I have your locket." He handed over the trinket.

Livvy's face light up. "Thank you, my lord, I am in your debt. 'Tis important to me. Errr... might I ask what happened last evening? I woke this morning, much later than is my habit, with no recollection of retiring to bed." Her expression reflecting her bafflement.

"You fell asleep in the chair, and Edie got you into bed. Simple as that." Philip left out his participation, going on to explain what had occurred with the secretary. The relief on Livvy's face was almost comical. "So that is done with, we shall not mention it again."

He changed the subject. "At the end of this week, I will be hosting three days of celebrations to welcome Sasha. A number of the guests will be staying here, and there will be all manner of entertainment, starting with a garden party on Friday afternoon. You will need several gowns. Mrs Challenor will assist you in that regard."

"No, thank you, my lord, but I do not believe that will be necessary. I shall either help with the preparations or, if that offends your sensibilities, return home." In her head, Livvy was already packing. This was her chance. She could get away before it was too late, resolutely ignoring the fact it already was.

"Livvy, for goodness sake when will you stop relegating

yourself to the kitchens? You are as entitled to join the fun as anyone else." He ignored her curled lip. "Besides, I discovered something when I was in York, which may change your mind. Would you like to know what?"

Livvy narrowed her eyes. "You have been investigating me?" She asked, her tone curiously flat. An ominous sign of which, had Sasha been around, he would have warned Philip.

"No, not investigating as such, but I was intrigued by your story and thought it wise to find out what I could about your family. You didn't seem to know much at all."

"You thought it *wise*? Wise for whom? Is this to establish whether I was suitable enough to bring up Sasha? A bit late now, my lord, I have been doing so for the past six years. You cannot turn back the clock and have the duke reply to my letters, sending someone to rescue his grandson from a life in a hovel." Livvy deliberately harked back to their first argument.

"Or, retrospectively provide enough wood, food, or clothing to keep us alive. I did that. Me. On my own. Of course, it would have been advantageous for Sasha to live the whole of his life in pampered comfort. He did not deserve to be abandoned. Thankfully, he does not appear to have suffered adversely and, I believe, will make a stronger duke for it. And that's another thing. When were you going to tell me, Sasha is, in fact, the duke? That your uncle died before anyone bothered to visit us at the cottage."

Livvy tried to control her temper, but it was a losing battle. Her life, everything she knew, felt like it was slowly upending, crumbling into a chaotic mess, and she didn't know whether she would ever be able to come to terms with it. After enjoying the luxury of Harrington Hall, the thought of returning to her cottage, although familiar, was no longer inviting — it was a hard life — but she couldn't stay here. It was as though she was adrift between two worlds. Then to hear he felt it necessary to investigate her.

She fixed him with a wintry stare. "You nobles are all the same. You think you can manipulate people without consequence. Well no more." Her voice dropping to a whisper. "You *investigated* me?" Dismayed, Livvy clutched her head and made to leave.

Philip moved to stand in her way. She tried to brush past, but his hand caught around her arm, drawing her towards him. Unable to help himself, he tilted her chin. He stared into her bewildered grey eyes, and something, deep within him, shattered.

"Livvy, please don't walk away. I thought discovering who your parents were might alleviate your sense of loss. I had no ulterior motive. I want what's best for Sasha and for you. You know you are welcome here for as long as you want, forever if you so choose. Why do we always end up arguing?" He held her gaze and could almost hear the debate going on in her head.

She drew a shuddering breath.

The silence stretched out.

"Because I am afraid. There, I've said it. Are you happy now?" Her voice rose. "I am afraid of leaving here, of saying goodbye to the only family I have, but I cannot stay. I am afraid of returning to the cottage where nothing is easy but is the only home I can remember. I am afraid, now I have lived here and experienced what the nobility enjoys, what Sasha will enjoy, I no longer fit anywhere, not here, not at the cottage. I'm afraid I have lost who I am."

Her cry fell into the quiet, and again she tried to leave.

Philip refused to let her go.

"Oh, Livvy."

Livvy's head shot up. There was something in his tone, it sounded like an endearment. She was about to speak, but he didn't give her the chance, grazing his lips over hers. She gulped, stunned by his touch.

Emboldened, Philip cupped the back of her head, entangling his fingers through her unruly hair, its heavy silkiness almost a caress.

Livvy remained motionless, completely flummoxed by what was happening and at a loss how to respond.

Philip lifted his head. "Livvy, I don't think you have the slightest notion what you do to me. You are the most contrary, intriguing, infuriating, bewitching woman I have ever met, and I am going to kiss you again."

CHAPTER ELEVEN

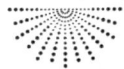

"*O*-oh..." was all she could summon up, when he bent his head, stealing her breath. His mouth moved lazily over hers, his lips warm and firm, and oh, so tender. Livvy felt a quiver ripple through her. Even acknowledging that this was not the most appropriate behaviour for either of them and could never happen again, she hadn't the will to stop it.

While Philip allowed the kiss to deepen, she experienced the most unusual sensation. One which had her pressing her body against his, had her arms sliding around his waist, and her fingers splaying against his back. The kiss went on and on. Livvy couldn't think, she couldn't hear, she forgot to breathe. Nothing mattered anymore, except that Philip was kissing her.

Although to Livvy it seemed hours had flown by, it was mere moments later when Philip broke their kiss. Both were gasping, faces flushed from the intensity of an affection neither had anticipated.

"Before you start panicking and trying to come up with ways of telling me that should not have happened, don't. I never do or say anything I don't mean. Come, sit with me. I must show you what I discovered."

Head whirling, Livvy allowed Philip to lead her over to the French windows. The view out over the landscaped grounds was as spectacular as always, but she didn't notice, barely able to think straight, never mind admire the gardens. Philip ushered her into one of the large wing-backed chairs and, reaching for the portfolio he had dropped on one of the side tables, removed several sheets covered with writing.

"Read this," he said. Handing them to Livvy, he took the chair next to her, watching as she scanned the words.

At first, all the lines blurred into one, but slowly she began to register details. She read every page through three times to be sure she understood. Placing them on the table, she looked at Philip.

"Do you expect me to believe I am related to the Earl of Rutland?" she demanded, incredulously.

"Whether you believe it or not, 'tis true. I have unequivocal proof your father was second cousin to Rutland and was also the son of a baron. He married and, from what I was able to determine passed away when you were quite young. Your mother died shortly before your eighth birthday."

Unbidden, the image of a dark-haired man swinging her in his arms popped into Livvy's head. *Was that her father?* The picture faded, and she forced herself to concentrate on what Philip was saying.

"Elinor Harrington was actually another of your father's cousins, as well as a friend of your mother's. In fact, from what I could establish, she introduced them. She and her husband, Tristram, took you in, although how you ended up in so small a home, I cannot fathom. I do have someone working on that."

Livvy shrugged. Until she came here, she considered the cottage substantial. It was certainly more sizeable than any of the other dwellings in the neighbourhood. What did they need with a big home? Nobody ever visited, and there had only been the four of them. She wondered why Elinor never clarified their relationship, but perhaps she assumed Livvy already knew.

"Mayhap they didn't require such opulence as this." She waved her hand around. "Mayhap they preferred a life away from the trappings. I presumed, owing to the duke's lack of interest in their well-being, they had been cut off. What does it matter anyway? They're dead." She concluded, bluntly.

"It matters because you inherited a title and some property. You are the sole remaining heir of the Baron de Courcy, your father, and apparently, there is a manor house some distance west of here."

Livvy stared at Philip, her mouth hanging open in shock. Pulling herself together, she asked the first thing that popped into her head.

"What about my cottage?"

"I daresay you can keep your cottage. How about we repair it, and keep it as somewhere we can run away to, when we are tired of being bossed about by the duke?"

Philip's words warmed her, implying something permanent had sprung up between them. *Ah, but did he only want her now because she was of the same class? Would he have kissed her, had he thought her no more than a servant?* He hadn't said he cared for her, simply that she bewitched him. That wasn't the same thing, was it? Did she dare ask? Well, she would have to. She couldn't allow this, whatever it was, to continue if she was naught but a dalliance to him.

"While that does sound inviting, I am left with questions."

"I had no doubt you would be. Ask away, 'tis not like you to be reticent."

"Had you not been aware of this..." flapping the sheets, "...would you have kissed me? Would you even contemplate what you just suggested? Are you... have you... did... what about...?" Livvy ran out of words, wary of asking the one question. His answer could grant her a lifetime of happiness or destroy the dream she hadn't even realised she wanted.

"Livvy, while I admit, when first we met, you were not someone I ever imagined liking, you have since become important to me. You are far too thin, far too small, far too independent and one of the most irritating women I have *ever* had the misfortune to deal with. You are also honest and loyal and loving and will do anything for anybody, often, I suspect, to your own detriment." Philip paused and leaning forward, ran a cool finger along her jawline, before stroking his thumb over her bottom lip.

Smiling gently, he continued. "You may have lost, in a few short years, more than most would lose in a lifetime, but it didn't crush you, merely made you stronger. Moreover, I don't want you to lose anything ever again. You may not be who my family would choose for me, you may not be very suitable, but you are all I want."

Livvy listened to his words. They weren't particularly romantic, and he hadn't told her he loved her. She couldn't shake the notion he was trying to convince himself more than convince her. Struggling to believe he truly harboured an affection for her, Livvy decided to wait and see.

She could not discount the whispers she had heard regarding a certain Lady Elise, who she knew was due to visit. Perhaps until things became clearer, it was it best to reserve her judgement.

"Pray tell me about these festivities you are planning." Livvy sought to re-direct the conversation before it became awkward.

Philip, realising her ploy, chose not to remark upon it and

instead explained the upcoming house party, adding, "…and as I have already stated, you must allow me to provide a wardrobe suitable for this occasion. While the gowns you own may be adequate for quiet country living, they are not acceptable for Society functions. No Livvy…" when she started to speak, "…I cannot, in all conscience, allow you to attend any gathering in my home, well Sasha's home, without a choice of new gowns. The gossips would have a field day. Please do not argue with me on this."

"I was going to say thank you, my lord," she murmured.

"Oh. In that case, we must begin at once, and how many times must I remind you? My name is Philip." He rang for Mrs Challenor, his housekeeper. Once apprised of the situation, the latter mentioned several garments, which could be altered to fit Livvy.

"Now then Miss, Edie and I are quite handy at sewing, and the gowns I have in mind will look like the latest fashion when we're through. You'll see. Come along, dear, let's go and have a look."

Shooing Livvy out of the library, Mrs Challenor led her up the stairs and right along to the end of the east wing of the Hall. "These are her ladyship's rooms, Lord Cranfield's Mama, well they were. She had so many dresses and was petite like you. After she died, they were cleaned, hung up in here and forgotten. I am certain some have never been worn."

The suite of rooms was cold and soulless.

Livvy had the impression the spirit of a long-dead woman lingered, observing this interloper who dared disturb the silence.

When the housekeeper opened the huge armoire, all thoughts of ghosts vanished. There were so many clothes in such beautiful shades. Warm, bright, shimmering colours.

Evening gowns, day dresses, riding habits, cloaks, shoes, wraps, pelisses, Livvy had never seen so many clothes.

Mrs Challenor lifted out gown after gown, nodding or shaking her head as she held each one against Livvy, eventually choosing what looked, to Livvy, like an inordinately large number. Happy with the selection, the housekeeper hurried the bewildered woman back to her bedchamber, getting her to try on every dress, pinning and tucking until she was satisfied.

Then she and Edie, who had been summoned to assist, gathered the great pile, and disappeared, leaving Livvy to question whether a storm had blown through her room.

The days leading up to the house party all merged into one. Livvy felt as though she was suddenly a child again. She spent every waking hour, being schooled in etiquette. How to eat, which knife to use, which glass to drink from, how to smile, how to use a fan, how to converse, which topics were acceptable and those to be avoided. It was exhausting, and Livvy questioned why she had ever agreed to this farce.

Nevertheless, she did not want to embarrass Philip, and made a concerted effort to push aside her naturally, sunny demeanour, becoming quiet, almost cheerless. Privately, the staff deliberated on whether Lord Cranfield would notice this change. Livvy was morphing into a shadow of the spirited young woman he had brought home less than a month ago.

Preparations continued all week. When the guests began to arrive on Friday afternoon, the house had taken on a festive air — fairly gleaming from top to bottom. Coach after coach rumbled into the courtyard, disgorging stylishly dressed ladies and soberly attired gentlemen.

After being escorted to their rooms to freshen up, the guests reappeared on the terrace to join the very young Duke of Albermarle, and his cousin the Marquis of Cranfield, for drinks — or in Sasha's case, fruit punch!

The warm summer air, slightly hazy as the day began to wane, encouraged the guests to wander around the grounds. The sound of their chatter and laughter drifted across the immaculate lawns. An abundance of food and wine was laid out on shining platters, while footmen and maids carried trays laden with drinks and delectable treats, to tempt the taste buds.

Livvy was nervous. Edie had come to help her dress and do her hair, something Livvy never required before, but was glad of this day. Her gown, although simple, was a vision in pale aqua silk, with a sheer overlay in a richer hue. The delicate materials appeared to merge when Livvy moved, flowing around her in gossamer iridescence, giving her an ethereal quality.

Her slippers matched the dress, for it transpired she shared a shoe size with the late marchioness, and although peculiar, wearing a dead woman's slippers, they fitted perfectly.

Edie brushed Livvy's hair until it shone, then fashioned it into an intricate style, curls piled on the top of her head leaving a few long ringlets to frame her face.

Livvy felt like a fool all dressed up. She was frightened to move in case she tore the fine fabric or tripped over. This translated into a young lady with a most noble bearing, who descended the stairs so slowly it was as though she floated.

Philip, who was chatting with some of his acquaintances, glanced around when an odd hush fell over the Great Hall. He sucked in a sharp breath at the sight of her. She looked like a princess from faraway lands.

Edie, who had come down behind her, handed Livvy her fan and whispered. "You look beautiful, Miss, never forget that. You're worth more than all this lot put together," she grinned at Livvy and dropped a wink. "Remember, they all require assistance getting dressed, and you can manage without... 'tis a leveller so 'tis."

Livvy whispered her thanks and stood a moment, unsure what to do or with whom she should speak.

Then Philip was there, offering her his arm, which she accepted gratefully.

"Thank you, my lord. I fear I will make a cake of myself before this evening is over," she muttered.

"Of course, you won't, Livvy, this is the world you were born into. Own it," he replied, quietly, squeezing her fingers, which felt icy through the lacy gloves.

The guests resumed their various conversations, and soon Livvy was drawn into a crowd of young men and women, who appeared genuinely interested in getting to know her.

Determined not to let Philip down, she answered their questions as honestly as she could without revealing anything much at all. She presumed they would not want to hear about domestic deprivation; it would likely offend their sensibilities.

She spoke in measured tones, and rarely smiled, prompting Jerome, one of the footmen, to make an aside to Edie, both agreeing they missed her vivacity — this new Livvy was far too withdrawn.

❦

Sometime during in the evening, Livvy — who hadn't eaten a morsel of food, terrified of dropping it down her dress, and had drunk maybe one or two glasses of punch more than she ought — while maintaining her enigmatic façade, began to relax.

She was chatting with a group of people and made the mistake of mentioning the cottage. The comment slipped out before Livvy could stop it, cursing her fickle tongue. Her listeners pressed her for more details, and she found herself sharing snippets of her life. She knew her words were running away with her, but these guests of Philip's seemed fascinated by her background. What was the harm?

Philip, catching a glimpse of her, was rendered momentarily speechless. His recent declaration aside, until this evening, he had never considered Livvy remotely beautiful, arresting maybe, but not beautiful. Tonight, this notion was swiftly diminishing yet, even as she took his breath away, something niggled at him.

Musing over what it could be, he registered that although Livvy's cheeks were a becoming pink and her hair was beginning to unwind itself from the elaborate style, her face bore no expression whatsoever.

Unbidden, Philip recalled her being markedly taciturn and coolly polite these last few days, quite unlike her normal irrepressible self. He saw Livvy incline her head graciously at those with whom she had been speaking and walk towards the terrace.

A thread of unease trickled through him. *What was going on in that head of hers?* He was about to follow her when a good friend hailed him, and the moment was lost.

❧

On the terrace, Livvy found Sasha and, heedless of the delicate gown she was wearing, sank onto the step next to him. They chatted for a time, and Livvy was glad she did not have to put on any airs and graces when with her brother. She was seeing less and less of him. His morning lessons and afternoon activities filled his day and, while this saddened her, she knew it to be inevitable.

She wasn't sure what was unfolding between her and Philip — if anything. He hadn't kissed her since that marvellous afternoon. Inexplicably, he seemed to have distanced himself. Maybe the whole thing had been an illusion.

Perhaps it was his way of distracting her from the abundance of information he had given her, the upset of the argument with Mr Stanley, or simply a momentary lapse in judgement. The thought she might be a mistake, sent a spasm of something painful in the region of Livvy's heart.

Sasha ran off to play with one or two of the other children who had accompanied their parents — madcap antics amusing an indulgent audience. Livvy sighed, wishing she was at liberty to hoist up her skirts and join in.

While she was sitting, her head resting against the door frame, she heard her name mentioned. Thinking someone was looking for her, Livvy stood and was about to announce her presence, to be brought up short by the speaker's next words.

. . .

"'Tis my belief, Philip is treating her as a charity case. 'Tis the duke who is important, that she is also here merely confirms his generosity. Moreover, everyone knows he is all but betrothed to Lady Elise." There were a few chuckles, then, "She will ensure the boy is shipped off to boarding school as soon as possible. She will not want a child interfering in her management of Harrington Hall. As for... what's her name again?" Apparently, Livvy's name was unimportant, because no one provided it. "She will be dispatched before Elise's luggage is unpacked."

"Will Cranfield marry Elise, do you think? This other woman is quite comely. A rival for his lordship's affections perchance?"

"Assuredly he will wed Elise. More likely he will keep the chit as his mistress. She ought to be grateful for whatever he offers."

If she moved, they would notice her, but how could she stay? Livvy was mortified, wishing she had never agreed to attend this stupid party. Unfortunately, her critics hadn't finished.

"The old duke's instructions were unequivocal, and Philip will do as duty requires. He loved his uncle. The man was a giant among the *ton* and well respected."

Livvy could not prevent her lip curling with disdain.

"Lady Elise will make an excellent wife. Furthermore, I have it on good authority," his tone becoming conspiratorial, "this de Courcy woman, while handsome of feature, has a sketchy past?"

There was a chorus of 'no, really, do tell,' his audience greedy for scurrilous gossip.

"I heard she lived in some dilapidated bothy, don't you

know, caring for the lad after his parents died. She might be a baroness now, but up until a month ago, what does anyone know of her? No, no, her background is dubious. Who knows what she's been up to? Likely she's been tipped more than once." The man's condescension indicated beggars in the street were more acceptable in Society than Livvy. "Her type will never be accepted by the *ton*."

Murmurs of agreement followed his comments.

Livvy was frozen in place. Heat scorched her cheeks while their words reverberated around her head. Is *that* what everyone was saying about her? She was some cheap whore, whom Philip had rescued, to be kept as his mistress. Was *that* what he meant when he talked about the cottage being a place of refuge? The place he would visit when he needed a quick tumble?

She made an odd sound, the noise attracting the attention of the small clique who at least had the decency to look uncomfortable. One of the ladies began to say something, to mitigate their words but Livvy straightened her shoulders, making herself as tall as possible — not easy when you are of petite stature.

In a dignified voice, she said, "Please, do not apologise for being honest. Since you are intrigued by my background, permit me to clarify one or two misconceptions. My house was a sizeable cottage, not a bothy. I worked hard every day from the age of four and ten to put food on the table, and ensured his Grace was never hungry or cold.

"The last duke, of whom you are so enamoured, ignored my pleas for help when his son was dying, so forgive me if I do not agree with your gushing sentiments. Had he one ounce of affection for his family, his grandson would never have been left to my tender and, yet obviously, deplorable mercies.

"So, no, we did not grow up in luxury. Our wealth came from things far less tangible but far more enduring. And, while I may not have had many comforts, at least I never used words to belittle another or be deliberately hurtful."

She dipped a curtsy and, head held high, swept out of the ballroom.

CHAPTER TWELVE

*L*ivvy flew along the terrace and into the library, dropping inelegantly into one of the huge leather chairs, contemplating what she had overhead. While the man's comments were insensitive, but she could not deny he was correct. She would never be accepted.

If Philip did want to... well she had no idea what he wanted, thus far he had not demonstrated any eagerness to share his intentions... his peers at social gatherings would probably, at the very least, ignore her.

She couldn't do that to him.

Philip had lived all his life in their rarefied world, and her presence would dismantle that illusion, leaving him vulnerable to their capricious whims. She knew how it felt to be ignored and forgotten. In her small world, it wasn't as painful as it would be for him.

Her decision made, Livvy heaved herself out of the chair. She stood for long moments breathing in the quiet beauty of this, her favourite room, then hurried up to her bedchamber. Divesting herself of her finery, Livvy laid the exquisite gown neatly on the bed, stroking her fingers over the silky material, a strange melancholy descending upon her.

Pushing it aside, she retrieved her case from under the bed, and placed her few items of clothing tidily within. The faded dresses looked cheap and inferior alongside the vibrant material of the gown she had just removed.

Livvy swallowed the sobs threatening to undermine her resolve. Sitting at the escritoire, she wrote two short letters, one of thanks to Philip and a loving goodbye to Sasha. She acknowledged it was cowardly not telling them face-to-face but knew they would try to dissuade her. It was less upsetting this way.

Gathering her cloak, she slipped on her old, worn boots and crept through the house to the domestic quarters, down the back stairs and towards the kitchens. She was nearly caught when Mr Warner and two of the footmen came along the corridor, but she ducked into the shadows, and they walked right passed her. Taking her courage in both hands, she rapped on the kitchen door, entering without waiting to be invited.

"Why, Miss Livvy, why on earth are you... wait... what are you doing dressed in those old clothes? Edie told me you looked... Livvy? What is going on?" Millie, hands on hips, eased her tones but pinned Livvy with her canny blue gaze.

"I'm sorry, Millie. I cannot stay. Things have... errr... taken an unexpected turn, and my presence here is no longer tenable. I have left both his lordship and his Grace a letter of explanation. No doubt Lord Cranfield will be furious, but this is as it should be. Sasha is settled, his life is here now, and mine is... well, mine isn't."

She sighed, and to the woman listening it seemed to come from a vast distance.

"Thank you, Millie for your kindness, for the kindness of all the staff, please let them know I will remain forever grateful for their acceptance of me." She threw caution to the winds and hugged the good-natured cook, who hesitated for a split-second, then wrapped her arms around Livvy's slender body.

"No need for me to say you shouldn't be leaving, your place is here with his lordship. You can't be thinking of going home? Why 'tis dark and the roads are not safe for a woman on her own. Wait until tomorrow, things are always better in the light of a new day," Millie entreated.

Livvy shook her head. "Do not worry, Millie, and please don't say anything. I will be vigilant and am used to looking after myself. As for his lordship, I am reliably informed he is destined for another, and I cannot stand on the sidelines while he takes a wife. It would break me."

The last uttered so quietly, Millie could not be certain she had heard correctly and, before she had the chance to say anymore or stop her, Livvy was gone.

"Oh, you poor dear. May God watch over you, my sweet." Millie's soft and prayerful farewell followed the young woman out of the door, as she hurried across the courtyard and down the long driveway to the gates. Livvy kept under the trees and out of sight of anyone who happened along. Unsure of the distance to her cottage, she *did* know in which direction it was, and once away from the estate, struck out at a steady pace.

Philip was ruminating over where Livvy had hidden herself. He had spent much of the party with Elise Sherrard, who was becoming increasingly possessive as the evening wore on, refusing to leave his side.

She was unable to disguise her distaste when someone questioned Philip about Livvy, or to stifle her revulsion when he clarified Sasha's life to date. Her long fingers clung to Philip's arm, digging in when he tried to move away. Her nails reminded him of talons, and he wondered why he ever imagined they could be happy together.

The memory of that brief kiss tormented him and, as the image of Livvy's expressionless face tugged at something in the depths of his soul, Philip surrendered. He was hopelessly, irrevocably in love with a self-possessed, obstinate, independent-minded young woman, who stampeded through his dreams and stalked his waking hours.

Nothing else mattered. Not even what Elise, what Society, expected of him. Nothing else mattered but to tell Livvy how he felt, in the hope she may possibly care for him, too.

When, at last, he was able to extricate himself from Elise, he went in search of Sasha who said he'd been talking to Livvy up on the step. The boy waved his hand in the direction of the terrace, where the doors to the great ballroom stood open allowing the mild evening air to waft across the grand space.

"But that was ages ago. Then I came out here with Roland and Jeffrey." He indicated the two brothers with whom he had been playing for the last hour or so. The state of their clothes testament to how much fun they were having.

Philip grinned. "Go on then away with you, 'tis clear you are having fun. If you see Livvy, please tell her I am looking for her."

Sasha nodded absently, running back to join his new friends. Philip observed him for a moment; glad the child was enjoying the evening. He strode back into the ballroom, scanning its length but there was no sign of Livvy.

He frowned.

It was as though she had vanished.

George, another of the household's footmen, appeared at his elbow.

"Are you looking for Miss Livvy?" George asked in undertones.

"I am, George. Have you seen her?"

"Not for a little while, but I do believe she overheard some tactless tittle-tattle. I happened by as she was taking them to task over it. She was politeness itself, but you could tell as she was perhaps, a trifle discomposed."

"With whom was she talking?"

George supplied the names of those involved, before continuing around the room, as though nothing was amiss. Philip, spotting the aforementioned, casually strolled towards them, stopping to chat with others on his way.

Lady Elise seized the opportunity to join him, slipping her arm through his, her air proprietary. Philip suppressed both a shudder and the urge to remove her hand. His unease over Livvy's whereabouts taking precedence over his supposed accord with this haughty lady whom, until a week ago, he considered making his wife.

"Featherstone, my good man, I understand you spoke to my..." he hesitated, searching for an acceptable word, "... ward, earlier this evening. Pray tell me, what was the gist of your conversation?" Philip enquired. There was no rancour in his voice, but his eyes demanded the truth.

"'Twas nothing, Cranfield. I merely pointed out to my acquaintances here that she has a questionable past and might be fun for a quick toss in the hay, but nothing more serious. Not *our* type at all. Hey, what!" He quipped with an arch grin, assuming Philip would be in agreement, his language somewhat ribald in the presence of ladies.

Featherstone's error in judgement was compounded when, possibly in attempt to absolve himself, he added... "Well you know what is said about people who eavesdrop."

Philip did not respond, regarding Featherstone with an unreadable expression.

Elise tugged on his arm. "Cranfield, come now, do not take on. Featherstone is being honest. You must see she is of no consequence, naught but some insignificant chit. 'Tis Alexander on whom you should be doting, not this de Courcy woman. Do I have a rival for your affections?" She smiled artlessly, expecting Philip to admit the subject of their discussion was nothing to him.

Philip stared at Elise. It was as though he could see her clearly for the first time, and he did not like the picture. Another face — pale, thin, and usually glowering at him — nudged at his subconscious, and he gave up the pretence.

"My dear Lady Elise, Miss de Courcy has spent the past six years looking after the heir to the dukedom with absolutely no assistance. She wrote to my uncle begging for help when my cousin and his wife were dying. She received no response and was left to bury the only two people she could recall being parents to her, as well as assume the care of their son. She was not even ten and four years old. What were you doing then, my lady? Living a life of cosseted affluence without a care in the world? Of course, you were, so please do not tell me Livvy is of no consequence. I refuse to discuss my private life in front of guests, but mayhap 'tis time we admitted our affection for each other is probably not enough to sustain a more formal arrangement. Oh, and it's His Grace to you. Now, I must ask you to excuse me."

With that, Philip unhooked Elise's arm from around his and walked away, leaving several people in his wake, mouths agape.

After a brief but fruitless check of the gardens and those rooms open to his guests, Philip was in a quandary. *Where was Livvy?* He dispatched Edie up to Livvy's bedchamber. The maid returned in a frantic hurry, clutching something in her hand.

"My lord, my lord, I think she might have gone, but I found these." Edie handed her master the two letters.

Philip noticed one was addressed to him and the other to Sasha. His heart sank, this could not be good. Going into the study, he sat behind the polished wooden desk, the desk where Livvy had uncovered the fraud perpetrated against him and began to read.

Dear Lord Cranfield

Thank you for your generous invitation to stay at Harrington Hall, which has been, for the most part, delightful. I acknowledge my leaving, in so cowardly a manner, will likely anger, or at least annoy you, but this evening has proved I cannot stay. Had I informed you of my decision, you might have felt obliged to change my mind.

We both know Sasha has settled in. He is young enough to accept his new circumstances with little difficulty, and I trust you will ensure his well-being at all times. As for whatever it was, we shared, I realise it was probably nothing more than a kindness. Our lives, our expectations are so far apart we can never find a middle ground... if that was ever your intention.

I understand you are to be wed to a very suitable lady, and I extend my congratulations. I beg you not to let her convince you to send Sasha to boarding school. He needs a loving family and a stable home life, somewhere he feels safe. After all, he's still very much a child.

I hope, eventually, you will forgive my hasty departure. I do believe this is for the best.

. . .

Oh, this letter is longer than I anticipated. Mayhap I am delaying in the hope this evening was just a nightmare. Then I see the beautiful dress and know it to be no dream.

Thank you again, Philip. I do not expect our paths to cross again, but I will cherish the memory of your kiss.

Livvy.

Philip read the missive twice. His temper flared at the same instant as he registered this was the first time Livvy had called him by his given name. There was no doubt about it; she was by far the most infuriating woman he had ever met. *Did she think his kiss meant nothing? That he would marry another after opening his heart to her?*

He paced around the study, muttering his ire, when unbidden a sentence popped into his head, '...you may not be who my family would choose for me, you may not be very suitable...' yes, he had concluded by saying she was all he wanted but hadn't actually told her how he felt. What he *had* told her was what everyone else would think... not particularly complimentary.

He should have told her, unequivocally, he loved her with every fibre of his being, and could not imagine his life without her. He hadn't opened the door of his heart to her. He had barely even cracked a window.

She thought he was going to marry Lady Elise, and presumed it was better to remove herself than be asked to leave by the new marchioness. Philip ground out an exasperated curse. Where had she gone? Surely, Livvy didn't think she could walk all the way back to her cottage? Of course, she did! When did miles of open countryside and the risk of being waylaid by ne'er-do-wells ever stop Miss Olivia de Courcy from doing anything? *Dash it all.*

He had a house full of guests. He couldn't leave, neither

could he let her walk through the night. Who knew what might befall her? He was ruminating over what to do when there was a knock on the door and, at his bidding, Millie stepped into the room.

"Come in, Millie, you need to see me? Is something amiss with the food?"

"Not in my kitchen, my lord, but I have something to confess. Miss Livvy came to see me to say goodbye."

His cook's tones bordered on contrite, which startled Philip. Millie was usually the one taking him to task. She had been with the Harrington family as long as he could remember and was held in the greatest awe by the other members of staff. Even Mr Edwards knew better than to cross her. In her turn, Millie was fiercely loyal, and protective of those under her wing and, it appeared, Livvy fell into that category.

"Tell me," he invited, wearily. Millie told him what Livvy had said, word for word. The young woman's departing comment solidifying his concern. His head in his hands, Philip tried to collect chaotic thoughts.

Millie patted him on the shoulder. "I think you know what you have to do, my lord. The question is, will you do it, or will you allow Society to dictate your happiness?" Nobody else could get away with such liberties, but Philip knew she was right. He heaved a huge sigh, which seemed to echo Livvy's of earlier.

"My lord, forgive me for stating the obvious, but if you love her, go after her. If you don't, let her go. 'Tis really that simple." Millie patted him again and then bustled out of the room, leaving him to his thoughts.

CHAPTER THIRTEEN

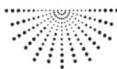

*P*hilip settled against the back of the chair, steepled his fingers together and considered his options. He could continue to play the polite host for the remainder of the evening and wait until the morning before going after Livvy. He could leave his guests to the tender mercies of his staff and go now — if he went on Hermes, he would doubtless catch her before she had walked very far. Or he could wait until the party was over and then follow her. He hadn't come to a decision when Sasha ran into the study.

"Cousin Philip is it true? Has Livvy gone?"

Taken aback that Sasha had found out so quickly, Philip nodded, and handed the child his sister's letter. It was much shorter than Philip's but far more loving. Livvy told Sasha how proud of him she was, and she knew he would be a most accomplished duke, but it was time she went home. Bessie, Claude, and the hens needed her, and it wasn't fair to expect Bernard to look after a home, which wasn't his. Moreover, there was plenty needed organising before the cooler weather arrived.

Sasha was upset but, curiously, not unduly surprised. "I

think she felt out of place, Cousin Philip. She spent most of her time with the staff, except when she was with me or in the evenings. I heard Jerome tell Edie it's because she doesn't think she should be here with us. I think that's silly, so did Jerome, he said Livvy was a…" he screwed up his little face as he tried to remember, "…that was it… a rare person who was able to re… relate to those on both sides of the door. I don't know which door he was talking about, but the others nodded."

Worried as he was, Philip bit back a grin at this and hugged Sasha. "Fret not my lad, as soon as this party is over, I will bring her home."

❧

Somewhere along a lonely road, Livvy, who had been walking for what seemed like forever, was tiring. Despite being used to long days of hard work, the last few were draining, and the party had taken an emotional toll. Her suitcase felt heavier with every step, and she was beginning to lag. Determined not to rest until she was home, Livvy forced herself to keep moving.

She was not so very far from the cottage when she heard a rustling in the bushes. Presuming it to be an animal, she ignored it but lengthened her stride. The noise seemed to follow, and when she stopped to listen, it also stopped.

"Who goes there?" She demanded, pleased she sounded vexed rather than scared. There was no reply "Probably a rabbit," she muttered, peering into the undergrowth, unable to discern anything in the gloom. The sun had long set, and although still the height of summer, it was well past twilight. The pale moon threw the shadows together, masking nature's true shapes.

Livvy drew her cloak around her, glad of its warmth. The

evening was mild, but the weight of the garment made her feel less vulnerable. She had scarcely taken two more steps when a figure loomed up in front of her, and she smothered a startled shriek.

"Who do we have here then... hmmm?" An unwelcome voice grated. "Miss Busybody herself. Well, well, well, all alone in the middle of nowhere. A young woman like yourself should know better. All manner of dastardly ruffians use darkness to cover their tracks. It would be an easy matter to hand you over and let *them* do the looking after."

His words sent a shiver of dread through Livvy, not that she had any intention of disclosing her alarm.

"Mr Stanley!" She countered, acerbically. "This is precisely what I might expect of you, skulking in the undergrowth. I am honoured your desperation to be in my company necessitates such furtive behaviour." She heard a sort of snarl. "You think you can scare me? You presume I am some simpering female who does not know how to take care of herself."

She marched forward, making sure she could see Mr Stanley from the corner of her eye, ready to run if needs be. Balling her free hand into a fist and calming her breathing, Livvy recalled the odd tussle in which she had become involved, shortly after her mother died. She had held her own against older, bigger boys, intent on stealing the few scraps of food she had been lucky enough to find. They had been far more desperate than this rat-faced man, so she didn't suspect he would present much of a problem.

He sidled up alongside her, his hand stretching out as though to grab her arm. Livvy sidestepped him and quickened her pace.

"You owe me, and I wager I can get a good price for you. A young woman, ripe for plucking. There's always those eager for fresh meat." Mr Stanley lunged. He snatched

Livvy's free hand and dragged her against him. His other hand grabbed her face, bony fingers digging into the soft skin of her cheek.

Unwilling to relinquish her suitcase, Livvy struggled to escape, but the disgraced secretary tightened his grip. She probably had one chance to break free from the man's clutches and it would need to be quick. *Make it count*, she instructed herself.

Drawing a long slow deep breath, Livvy emptied her mind and concentrated. Pivoting abruptly, she bent her knee and aimed it with all the force she could muster at the secretary's groin, simultaneously biting his hand in the sensitive webbing between thumb and forefinger. Mr Stanley howled in pain and released his hold. Delivering a swift, and vicious kick to his ankle, Livvy hoisted her skirts and fled as though the devil himself was after her.

"You little vixen! Wait until I get my hands on you." Mr Stanley spat the words, agony jabbing through him. He sucked on his hand, tasting his own blood. "God's teeth, but you are a bitch. When I catch you, you will rue the day you were born!" He yelled, hobbling after his prey.

Livvy ran and didn't look back. She dodged among the trees, her suitcase swinging wildly, her cloak and hair streaming out behind her. The moon provided enough light that she didn't trip on an upturned root or rabbit hole. *Please, let me get home*, she prayed, knowing Bernard was there and would protect her.

Mr Stanley, ignoring his throbbing body, took off in hot pursuit.

❧

Philip was gaining on them, his trusty stallion covering the ground far more quickly than the two on foot. He tried to do his duty, but concern for Livvy outweighed his need to be polite. He had made a brief speech in which he thanked everyone for attending and hoped they were having a splendid evening. Without actually saying so, he gave the impression he would continue to mingle, asking his guests to make sure they introduced themselves to Alexander, the new Duke of Albermarle.

He circulated for a while, chatting with friends, before slipping away to the stables. An earlier message to his groom, meant Hercules was already saddled. Philip had mounted the stallion and was galloping down the road almost before his groom realised his master had arrived in the stables.

On the still night air, any sound carried a long way. Philip had been riding for about forty minutes when he heard an argument not far in front of him. Slowing Hercules to a walk, he listened intently, catching Mr Stanley's shout of pain, his subsequent threat, and the thud of heavy footsteps.

Ahead, Livvy was flying like the wind along the edge of the road, uncaring now, her whole being focused on getting to Rose Cottage. She couldn't remember how far it was, but it felt like an age since she left Harrington Hall. Recognisable landmarks appeared, spurring her on. She turned onto the winding track leading to her cottage, safety almost within sight.

Disaster struck.

Too late, she noticed a deep rut in the road and, in trying to avoid it, misstepped.

Livvy fell headlong, slamming into the ground, her suit-case skidding into the hedgerow, the impact knocking the wind out of her. Stunned, she lay in the dust, trying to get her breath back. The next few minutes unfolded in slow motion.

Mr Stanley reared over her cackling with glee, rubbing his hands together.

"I said you would pay, and there's no one to save you now. Get up, you little hellcat!" He seized her by the hair and yanked her upright. "Don't even think about screaming until I hand you over. They don't mind an unwilling victim," he hissed, holding something very sharp against her ribs.

Presuming this to be a knife, Livvy succumbed to her escalating panic. Defying his threat, she started to scream, the sound slicing through the stillness.

"Shut. Up!" Mr Stanley swung the fist in which he held the knife, striking her with savage brutality across the face. The blow caught the same spot on her cheek where the door had hit her, the day she met Philip.

Pain lanced through Livvy's skull, lights danced in her vision and everything started to recede. Her legs buckled, and she felt herself crumpling to the dirt. The last thing she saw was a horse approaching.

Impossible.

Then everything went black.

Philip arrived on the scene in time to witness Mr Stanley hit Livvy. Fury howled through him, and he was off Hercules in an instant, tackling the man to the dirt, getting in several well-placed blows with ruthless fists.

"You would raise your hand to a woman?" he roared. "You cowardly piece of filth. I am ashamed to think you were ever in my employ. How dare you?" He lifted the man bodily off the ground by the scruff of his collar and all but threw him into the hedge. "I suggest you take yourself as far away as you can. Otherwise I might be tempted to inform these ruffians with whom you were quick to threaten Miss Livvy, that you have reneged on your bargain and let them deal with you. Go!"

For one tension-filled moment, it looked as though Mr Stanley might attack Philip, but his erstwhile employer had the advantage of youth, height, and muscle. The older man, an inveterate coward when faced with someone less easily intimidated, limped away ranting malevolently.

Philip, expelling an angry breath, monitored the man's progress until he was out of sight. Hopefully, that was the last they would see of Mr Stanley.

His stallion's soft whinny brought Philip's attention back to Livvy, who lay motionless in a heap on the track. Spying her suitcase, Philip hitched it to the saddle and then scooped up Livvy. He led Hercules to a convenient fence where, without relinquishing his hold, he remounted. Clicking the horse into a smooth canter, the trio reached the cottage shortly thereafter.

Banging on the front door, Philip yelled for Bernard. The gardener appeared moments later, his tired face reflecting his shock at this untimely interruption to his slumber.

"Miss Livvy has been hurt. I'm taking her to her bedchamber. Please bring a bowl of water and a cloth." With that, Philip was up the stairs and into Livvy's room in a heartbeat. Despite the motion of the horse, she hadn't regained consciousness, causing Philip concern.

Settling her carefully on the faded coverlet, he cupped her cheek with a gentle hand. "Livvy. Livvy, wake up, my love, you're safe at home."

To his relief, she reacted. Shifting slightly, she pushed

away his hand, muttering something about dastardly deeds and conniving curs, but nothing of any real sense.

"Livvy!" He raised his voice and stroked her face, which was smudged with dirt. He noted several bruises, lurid against her pale skin. Anger at the man who inflicted them roiled through him.

Bernard brought in a bowl and some squares of cloth. Gently, Philip cleaned away the mud, checking to see whether the blow had split her lip or the inside of her cheek. He was pleased to discover it hadn't but surmised she would sport a sizeable black eye by the morning.

Philip was finishing his ministrations, when Livvy stirred.

The two men held their breath.

She opened her eyes.

CHAPTER FOURTEEN

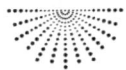

"*L*ivvy?"

Livvy gazed at Philip. Her eyes flicked to Bernard, then swung back to Philip, her brow creasing in confusion.

"How... where am... did you... what?" She shook her head, trying to make her tongue follow instructions, and promptly stopped. The movement made her dizzy. "Urrgghhh... feel sick..."

Faster than Philip believed it possible for his gardener to move, Bernard tossed the water from the bowl out of the window and had it under Livvy's chin. Just in time, for she was violently sick.

"Oh no... so sorry... can't seem to..." She was sick again.

"Hush, sweetheart. Don't worry, we shall deal with everything in the morning." Philip comforted her.

Bernard removed the bowl, returning moments later with a glass of water. Livvy rinsed her mouth, handed back the glass and started to speak. It proved too hard, and she slipped back into oblivion.

"I'll sit with her, Bernard. She probably ought not to be

left alone. I apologise for this disturbance. Go, find your bed, I will tell you about it on the morrow."

Bernard thanked him with a weary grin and left the room.

Philip sat beside the bed holding Livvy's hand. He couldn't let her go; eternally thankful he hadn't waited until the morning to follow her. Her likely fate, had Stanley not been thwarted, chilled him to the bone. Making himself comfortable in the chair, Philip closed his eyes and within minutes was fast asleep.

❧

It was still dark when he was jolted awake by strangled yells. Arms flailing, Livvy was thrashing on the bed, apparently fending off an unseen assailant, her terror making Philip's heart lurch.

"Hush, Livvy, no need to be afraid. You're safe with me." He grasped her arms and, acting on instinct, sank onto the bed, gathering her into his embrace.

Her cries subsided to unintelligible ramblings and, unconsciously, she relaxed against him, nudging her head until it was under his chin. One arm fell gracefully across his waist, her fingers coming to rest on the rise of his hip.

His cheek pillowed on Livvy's head, Philip's nose caught the scent of her hair. It reminded him of spring blossoms and sunshine. Her wayward curls, velvety soft. It was a struggle not to entwine his fingers through her luxuriant tresses, while he kissed her frustratingly enticing lips.

Sighing, he kicked off his boots and drew up the covers. Satisfied Livvy was comfortable, Philip fell back into slumber.

❧

Livvy was dreaming.

Dreaming of being romanced.

Her suitor was exceptionally tall. While not particularly handsome, his features were compelling, and he exuded charisma. Unruly dark-blond hair, slightly longer than was fashionable, brushed the collar of an open-necked, snowy-white shirt barely tucked into his buckskins. Chocolate brown lashes framed arresting green eyes, and his gaze sent heat all the way to her toes.

Warm, she was too warm.

Livvy tried to shove back the bedcovers but was hindered by an unseen weight. Grumbling to herself, she tried again, to have her efforts halted by a cool hand clamping around her wrist. Fear clawed at her mind, a shriek bubbling up.

She braved a peek, her gaze colliding with the same green eyes of her dream.

Livvy's scream died in her throat. She stared, blinked, and stared again. Closing her eyes, she shook her head as though to clear her vision, took a breath, and opened them again. The eyes hadn't moved, and the hand still grasped her wrist.

A voice spoke. "It's me, Livvy, Philip."

Those lovely rich tones, she must still be asleep.

"Philip?" She murmured drowsily... *wait... what?* Instantly wide awake, she squirmed around, realising she was all but lying on top of him. "Philip! What the *hell* are you doing in my bedchamber... on my... *in my bed?*" She squawked the last few words, mortified this man, the man it appeared she had been dreaming about — *oh God, could it get any worse?* — was in her bed.

"You were having nightmares. This seemed the best way

to calm you." Philip grinned, unabashed. "Did you know you talk in your sleep?"

Livvy flushed bright red… *so yes, it probably could get worse, dammit.*

"Errr… hmm… well…" Livvy ground to a halt. She had no recollection of how he came to be there or what had transpired after Mr Stanley hit her. Philip was probably furious with her for running away, and presumably, he had rescued her — *again.*

She rubbed her forehead distractedly and made to get up. Her right cheek ached, and her head felt peculiar. The latter likely the result of Mr Stanley's fist and sleeping too long. Pushing back the covers, she was relieved to see they were both fully dressed.

"Where do you think you're going, madam?" Philip enquired, his tones silky, a dangerous sign.

"To get washed and changed. It appears I slept in my clothes. Thank you for bringing me home. I errr… anyway, thank you. I'm sure you have more important things to be doing than lying in my bed."

"Can't think of anything," he said lazily, an odd glint in his eye.

Livvy didn't know what to do. This was way beyond her experience. "Don't you have a house full of guests and a very important lady to whom you should be playing host?" she groused, sullenly.

"None of your concern. You left, remember."

"Yes, I did, and now you ought to do the same. Your own life awaits. Thank you for bringing me here. I shall thank Bernard and let him know his services are no longer required," her tone was bleak. She slid away from him, off the bed and out of the door.

. . .

Philip groaned. She really knew how to aggravate him.

He got up, stretched, and strolled downstairs. Bernard was in the garden, tending to the vegetables. The sun shone, and the sky was blue.

It was a perfect summer's day, except for the black cloud hanging over him in the shape of Lady Olivia de Courcy.

❧

Livvy reappeared, washed and in a fresh gown or rather one of her old, shabby dresses, more patches than material, flushing a little when Philip ran his eye over it. She shrugged but said nothing, walking past him, out of the door and through the garden to the field, where Bessie and Claude stood quietly chewing the grass. They turned when she called their names, ambling over to be petted. She stood for a moment inhaling their warm scent, stroking their noses.

Without a backwards glance, she strode out onto the moor, revelling in the utter nothingness. Loving the feel of the cool grass between her bare toes — shoes not required here. The wild, untamed landscape offered a peace nowhere else on earth could. *Well…* no, she pushed that thought aside. *Don't even think it, Livvy,* she chided herself, *he's not for you.* A little grassy mound offered a makeshift perch and Livvy sat down, her thoughts whirling.

She had been sitting scant minutes when she heard footsteps. A trickle of fear threaded through her; she was alone again. Logic reasserted itself, and she turned to see Philip striding towards her, his face like thunder.

"How *dare* you walk away from me? After everything you put me through last evening, you think you can walk away without explanation? *It. Is. Not. Acceptable!*" Philip bellowed.

His fear over what might have happened at the hands of Mr Stanley, his sense of loss that she had felt the need to flee, and his despair when he saw her crumpled in the roadway, coalesced into one steaming bout of temper.

Livvy leapt to her feet, not cowed in the slightest. "What, pray, *is* acceptable to you? Is it acceptable to kiss me and tell me I am all you ever want, then introduce me to your intended wife?" She raged. "What *am* I to you? Someone who might prove to be a good tumble? Someone you can hide away in a hovel, visiting when your perfect wife spurns your advances? The pathetic chit who should be grateful for whatever the lord of the manor throws at her?"

She was bristling with fury. "Did you stop to think about my feelings in all this? Did it *ever* occur to you that to see you wed another would break my heart? *Of course*, it didn't. You noblemen are all the same, taking until we are of no more use, then tossing us aside, forever ignored and neglected. Oh, no, my lord, you will *not* dangle temptation in front of me then snatch it away. You can keep it. Go away and leave me to my life." She flung her arm in the direction of Harrington Hall.

Tears were coursing down Livvy's cheeks, but she was unaware she was crying.

Philip was glaring at her, his brows knitted, and she braced herself for the backlash.

It never came.

Instead, he took two steps towards her, seized her hand, hauled her against him and kissed her until the world stopped spinning.

Shaken, Livvy held herself rigid, determined not to bend

to his will, but the longer he kissed her, the less she was able to remember why she was angry.

His lips, firm and cool, invited her to open to him, while his embrace tightened, moulding her to his burly frame. Whimpering softly, Livvy couldn't stop her arms circling him, surrendering under the potency of his touch as their kiss went on and on and on.

With one finger, Philip stroked her jawline, tracing the delicate skin of her throat to the hollow at the base of her neck, feeling the erratic rhythm of her pulse. His hand skimmed over her shoulder, trailing down her spine, to span her waist.

Livvy's heart was drumming so fast, she half expected it to explode as she lost all awareness of time and place.

Philip broke their kiss. They were both gasping, and Livvy was finding it hard to remain upright. Her legs had no strength in them.

"W-what was that for?" She stammered, staring up at him, her expression uneasy, not daring to trust.

"You think I would break your heart?" His tone was one of amazement, her words giving him hope. "Olivia de Courcy, I would never wish to break your heart, I wish to cherish it. My greatest desire is to marry you, and if I cannot, if you deny me, I will never marry at all."

Confounded, she held his gaze. Tempestuous grey on optimistic green. "But what of Lady Elise?" A tinge of bitterness in her voice.

"I admit she was the one I was supposed to marry. Our families thought we would make a good match."

"You would," she whispered, brokenly, dropping her eyes. "I am no one's idea of a good match."

"You are *my* idea of the perfect match. I do not want a

wife who agrees with everything I do or say. I cannot imagine how boring my days would be, should the woman I wed make it her business to ensure my life is like a millpond — not a ripple to be seen.

"I want a wife who will challenge, argue, harass, push, pull, and most of all love me with all my faults. Who will not try to turn me into someone else. Who likes to run barefoot through the grass, who loves to laugh, who helps and encourages rather than demeans and belittles. Who treats others with dignity and respect, whatever their station in life.

"Most of all I want a tiny, dark-haired, grey-eyed, fiery little hoyden to love me as much as I love her."

Livvy listened to his candid words, heard the sincerity in his voice, but when he came to the last, her head shot up and she gaped at him.

"Y-you love me?"

"Of course, I do, you goose. I don't chase halfway across the countryside in the middle of the night for just anyone, you know."

"I never expected you to love me. To have an affection for me, would have been enough."

She hesitated.

"No, that is a fallacy. Affection would never be enough. I want to be the one you think of each morning when you wake. The one you want in your arms every night. You must understand, I can never share you. I have lost too much, and that you might leave me to bed another would destroy me. I want all of you or nothing at all. Moreover, if you truly want me as your wife, your peers will likely snub you. Can you live with that? I could not bear it if you came to see me as the reason for their disdain. Your rejection would be worse than a slow, painful death."

She shivered, aware how easily what seemed almost within reach might slip away. "Philip, I love you more than life itself, but you *have* to be sure. You ha—"

Her plea was cut short when Philip recaptured her lips.

Allowing their smouldering passion to flare, Philip kissed Livvy into joyful delirium. Under a glorious summer sky, all her worries, uncertainties and confusion were doused, as Philip convinced Livvy his heart was forever hers and, often what is least expected, is precisely what you need.

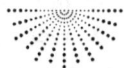

A YEAR LATER

$\mathcal{L}$ady Olivia Cranfield stood on the terrace of a sprawling manor house nestled deep in the wilds of Yorkshire, contemplating all that had happened over the past year. It was mid-September, the air was cool and the days shortening, but the mellow light was utterly magical and the landscape, breathtaking.

The day after that fateful party, Lady Elise declared she had no mind to stagnate in the countryside. London was too, *too* exciting and marriage to Lord Cranfield had never been a serious consideration anyway. She returned to the city, immediately becoming the darling of many a titled bachelor.

Mr Stanley disappeared. His name cropped up several months later when news filtered through, reporting he had been killed during a brawl outside a seedy tavern in one of the local port towns. While no one wished him dead, that he no longer posed a threat came as a relief to all.

The cottage, dutifully restored, was thriving. Bernard, who had been with the Harrington family for almost fifty years, was offered it as a living. He accepted gratefully, enjoying a quieter life, and Livvy visited frequently.

Philip refused to countenance a long betrothal. He and Livvy were married as soon as was possible, after which he brought her here, to the de Courcy ancestral home. Save the skeleton staff who had maintained it — all expenses covered by the Earl of Rutland — Braithwaite Park had not been lived in for over ten years. Now, it was their haven. A sanctuary from all the humdrum nonsense of their everyday world, a place of escape and they cherished its isolation.

When Livvy first walked through the house, long-forgotten memories flooded in. This was where the tall dark-haired gentleman swung her around. She had found his portrait hanging in the gallery, alongside that of his wife who was wearing the locket, and Livvy finally allowed herself to remember her mother.

Philip had been unable to discover why and how Livvy ended up on the streets, but she no longer wanted to know. She had survived, and that was enough. While there were tears for all she had lost, she was glad to be able to say good-bye. To let go of the past and begin her new life with Philip, who never allowed the sun to set without telling her, in word and deed, how much he loved her. A sentiment she recipro-cated in kind.

. . .

Currently, Sasha was staying with Roland and Jeffrey — the brothers he met at that same party. His friendship with these two had encouraged him to ask whether he might be allowed to attend Eton with them, and he would begin his schooling there after Christmas. Livvy would miss her brother but was pleased Sasha felt ready to make such a choice, and he was very excited. His life already being mapped out.

❦

Almost for the first time since their marriage, it was just Philip and her, and Livvy relished the intimacy. While she soaked in the ever-changing view, the sound of approaching footsteps reached her ears, and she became aware of someone entering the room. Livvy knew who it was without looking, her heart already lifting, a smile curving her lips.

"Good evening, Livvy. I thought I might find you here." Philip spoke quietly, but the rich timbre of his voice resonated all the way through her, as it did every time he spoke.

"I could stand here all day and never tire of it," waving her hand towards the moors, as she canted her head to look into her husband's beloved face. "Have you satisfied yourself the stewards have everything under control?" She enquired, archly.

Philip had been in meetings all day with the estate's managers, needing to ensure all was organised for the long winter months, despite his wife's assertion they had been managing perfectly well without him for over a decade.

Grinning at her expression, he replied. "Yes, thank you. We are all but finished. Mayhap by luncheon tomorrow it will be concluded." He moved to stand behind his wife of almost a year, drawing her close, her back to his chest and kissed the top of her head. Livvy relaxed against him, breathing in his familiar scent, heat beginning to coil through her.

"How are you feeling, love?" Although an apparently innocuous question, a couple of weeks before they left Harrington Hall, the family doctor had confirmed what Livvy already suspected, and Philip was inclined to worry.

"I am fine, Philip, you must stop coddling me." Her smile telling him she loved that he did. Glancing down, Livvy absently stroked her stomach, which had begun to swell. Philip placed his hand over hers, and the love in his gaze prompted Livvy to wish they dared flout convention so he could assuage the desire scorching through her, right here in the open doorway.

"Kiss me." she beseeched. Turning in his embrace, inquisitive fingers pushed aside his coat, searching under his waistcoat, feeling the muscles flexing.

A chuckle rumbled through him. "I see, it's like that is it, you have become very demanding of late."

"I am carrying your child, so I am allowed. Now shut up and kiss me." She growled.

The chuckle became outright laughter, and Philip bent his lips to hers, kissing her until she could hardly stand.

"Much better," she gasped when, eventually, he lifted his head.

"I am at your service, my love."

Livvy giggled when Philip waggled his eyebrows comically.

He took her hand. "Come on inside, the day cools, and it would not do to take a chill."

Reluctantly, Livvy dragged herself away from the panorama, vivid greens fading to subtle greys in the waning light.

. . .

Shortly thereafter, Mr Sargeant, the butler, came to serve drinks and confirm dinner would be served within the hour. The couple chatted about this and that, sharing their day, planning what they might do for the last week of their time at Braithwaite.

❦

Livvy and Philip were in their bedchamber, smouldering ardour cooled although perhaps not wholly satiated. Philip appeared to be fast asleep, but Livvy found herself unable to settle. Rather than disturb her husband by tossing restlessly, she got up.

Shrugging into Philip's discarded shirt, Livvy curled up in one of the chairs alongside the hearth, tucked a blanket over her knees, and opened her book. Within seconds she was absorbed by the tale therein, content to read by the light of a single candle and the glow from the fire.

Engrossed in the story, Livvy was unaware Philip had woken as soon as she left the bed. As he studied her in the flickering light, his dream from so long ago, popped into his head.

His shirt had slipped off one of her shoulders, exposing the creamy rise of her breast. Her hair, in riotous disarray from their lovemaking, spilled down her back, dark rivulets over white cotton. The inarticulate sound he tried to swallow had her twisting around in the seat. Her face shadowed, luminous grey eyes reflecting the flames leaping in the grate.

She held his gaze, running her tongue over suddenly dry lips. The blaze he never failed to kindle, reigniting. Philip was out of bed and beside her in an instant.

"I did not mean to wake you," she murmured. He took her hand and pulled her up from the chair, kissing her nose, her forehead and behind her ear, at the same time as he threaded cool fingers through her hair, eliciting all manner of delicious sensations.

"I always know when you are not beside me." He shuddered when her hands trailed over his naked body, cold fingers taunting fevered flesh. "Ooof, your hands are cold."

"Well warm them up." Livvy swayed against him in invitation.

Philip needed no second bidding.

His lips stole hers in a searing kiss, while turbulent heat spiralled through her.

The shirt, once alluring, now hampered his seduction and was tossed aside with more haste than care. Livvy trembled, her body begging for his touch, a soft moan escaping when his fingers traced her shape, seeking her most sensitive parts.

Philip lifted his wife, carrying her to their bed, where he made intoxicatingly passionate, yet exquisitely tender love to her until, as the moon began its slow descent, they fell asleep in each other's arms, limbs delightfully entangled.

Two days later, when all estate business was complete, the couple decided to take a carriage ride out to the ruins of an old Cistercian priory. Philip, discovering Livvy was fascinated by anything to do with the past, had made it his business to explore as many historical monuments as possible during their sojourn at Braithwaite.

Their sumptuous picnic eaten and remains tidied away, they were propped against a low wall, watching swallows gather for their long journey south.

It was a sheltered spot.

The sun was warm, and all was peaceful.

After several moments of quiet, Philip took Livvy's hand. "My darling Livvy, a year ago today you made me happier than I ever dreamed possible by standing in front of God and our families and binding yourself to me. You blew into my life in *the* most unexpected manner and turned it upside down. My fiery hoyden, I never imagined someone so spirited, so headstrong, and so utterly exasperating would tame my heart. From the moment you called me a sanctimonious fatwit to the day I draw my last breath, it has been, and will always be, in your hands. On this, the anniversary of our wedding day, I once again pledge my life to yours."

Livvy stared at Philip while he spoke, drowning in the fathomless depths of his eyes. The words she wanted to say stuck in her throat as ridiculous tears formed. She blinked furiously, determined not to cry, blaming her pregnancy for such feminine nonsense.

Philip stroked a thumb under one eye, catching a traitorous tear as it trickled over her sooty lashes.

"I'm sorry, love. I did not intend to make you cry."

"Pay no mind, 'tis just me being overly sentimental." She steadied herself. "Philip, it took me a little while to recognise my feelings were more than simple gratitude for the kindness you showed Sasha and me. I was so angry and disillusioned with the nobility and all it stood for, that to trust anyone not to let me, to let Sasha, down again, was impossible. Then you came, and you refused to allow me to hide behind my prejudice and my insecurities.

"Nothing could have prepared me for the moment I realised I loved you. It was as though I walked on shifting sands. What I believed to be certain, dissolved into something far less tangible, and it terrified me. I was used to being in charge and to relinquish any part of me to another felt like a betrayal. But you wouldn't let me go, even when I ran, you found me. My dearest love, when you rescued me, you rescued my heart. You breathed life back into me and made me yours for eternity.

"On this, the anniversary of the first day of the rest of my life, I affirm that love and vow always to be your fiery hoyden."

Livvy gripped Philip's left hand, stroking her fingers over the signet ring she had slipped on his third finger one year ago, her voice cracking with the strength of her emotions.

With his right hand, Philip cupped her cheek, before sliding his fingers into her lustrous hair and, bringing her lips to his.

In the golden warmth of a September afternoon, the sky an azure canopy, Livvy and Philip celebrated their unexpected, yet abiding love, with a passion as fervent as the day they first dared open their hearts.

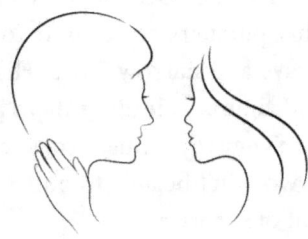

EXCERPT FROM LUCK BE A PIRATE

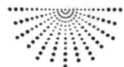

PART OF A REGENCY DUET

LONDON ~ NOVEMBER 1819

Kennet Alexson dodged along the murky streets, his breath coming in short bursts. He knew this district like the back of his hand, giving him a slight edge, but his pursuers were used to hunting people down dark alleyways and narrow lanes. His only advantage was, they had no idea he was leading them into a trap. They wouldn't give up. They presumed they could catch him unawares, that he wouldn't be able to outrun them, that they still had an element of surprise.

Little did they realise, if caught, surprise would be the element he turned on them.

Slipping between buildings in the squalid backstreets, Kennet paused, listening, and sniffing the air much like a dog sniffs out sausages. He could smell the unwashed odour of their bodies and hear the slap of bare feet on the cobbles. Needing to catch his breath, he sank to the ground completely obscured by the shadows.

Dammit all to hell.

Given their pathetic reasoning, he was flabbergasted they

had bothered to track him down. They surely had been drinking too much tainted rum.

It was more than two years since he had slipped away from the Lucky Doubloon, while the sloop was undergoing lengthy yet vital repairs in a Caribbean shipyard, after a run in with the French navy.

News had filtered through to him, via the privateers' network, that someone with whom he was once intimate had been held captive for many years. She had finally escaped, but Kennet was seized by an inexplicable compulsion to make sure, to see for himself that she was indeed safe and protected. She remained important to him, despite their decades apart.

He had explained all this to his quartermaster, couching it in far less emotional terms and blurring over the odd detail, before handing over the captaincy of the vessel. That same night, he had departed under cover of darkness so as not to alert either his, somewhat volatile, crew or the customs men patrolling the docks.

In Kennet's mind, that was the end of their association. He didn't take anything other than the clothes he was wearing and some coin. Neither did he divulge their where-abouts when intercepted and questioned by three naval officers — intent on breaking a racketeering ring — who tried to prevent him from boarding a ship bound for London. Kennet convinced his interrogators he was merely a sailor, fallen on hard times, trying to work passage back to England to his family.

By the time he disembarked at the Surrey Commercial Docks in Rotherhithe, he was weary of life at sea. To put down roots, to have a bed that didn't sway, to eat food that wasn't crawling with weevils, was suddenly, and unexpect-edly, appealing.

He had found a place to lay his head. Not particularly clean or comfortable, but after the Lucky Doubloon, sheer luxury — ignoring the fact you still had to sleep with a dagger at your fingertips. Next, he needed a job, eventually securing employment as a coal whipper on the docks, shifting coal from the colliers into lighters and barges.

It wasn't long before he was promoted — if one could call it that — to coal porter, part of a gang of brawny dockhands who unloaded coal either from ships at the wharf side or from the lighters and barges. This latter job also involved delivery of coal to residential customers, and Kennet quickly became familiar with the streets of London, a knowledge that would serve him well in the not too distant future.

He had been in England about six months when his luck changed again. Archie Miller, one of the coal whippers with whom he was friendly, landed a new job, and worse, no longer stopped in at the Windy Sail — a less than reputable tavern not far from the docks — for a pint on his way home from work.

When Kennet eventually caught up with him, in early October, Archie explained he had been offered a position at Trentams, one of the fastest growing shipyards. It was a great opportunity and, as Archie said, it was make or break for him.

"Sybs'll leave me if I don't get a grip o' myself. I love the booze, but I love 'er more. Got this job by the kindness of an actual Lady, so I did. You should come by, see whether they're hiring."

"They won't take on the likes of me, Archie. You know my background." Kennet had spilled his tale during one drunken afternoon not long after they met, but Archie hadn't held it against him, saying everyone had their secrets.

"I dunno. Mr Drummond is a decent sort, and fair. With what you know you'd prob'ly be an asset to them, you could warn 'em of the wily ways of pirates. Y'know, tell 'em where ships are likely to be raided. I think it'd be mutually beneficial." His tones a little haughty — rubbing shoulders with the merchant class had clearly enhanced Archie's vocabulary. Kennet chuckled and said he would think about it.

Three weeks later, an opportunity presented itself, and he approached Mr Holland, the master shipwright. Outlining his skills, Kennet admitted he had spent some years aboard a pirate sloop, hounding shipping up and down the Americas.

Taken by the man's honesty and obvious ability, Mr Holland spoke with Hugh Drummond, the owner of Trentams. Mr Drummond could see the sense in having someone who knew how pirates schemed, but would only agree to a trial period initially, and under strict supervision.

Kennet jumped at the offer, and had quickly proved himself a capable employee. His time on the Lucky Doubloon standing him in good stead with the particulars of ship building and repairs, not to mention he was a seasoned sailor. Before long, his probation was lifted, and he never gave Mr Drummond the slightest reason to regret his decision.

That was nigh on a year past and in that time, there had been no inkling of the trouble stalking him. Then not quite two months ago, everything he had worked for, everything he held dear was suddenly in grave jeopardy.

His old crew had tracked him to London, why they felt the need was beyond him — they had his ship, not to mention the treasure they'd plundered. If they found out where he worked, everyone at Trentams was at risk and that was something he refused to have on his conscience, for more reasons than the obvious.

There was also Lynette.

ABOUT THE AUTHOR

Rosie Chapel lives in Perth, Australia with her hubby and three furkids. When not writing, she loves catching up with friends, burying herself in a book (or three), discovering the wonders of Western Australia, or — and the best — a quiet evening at home with her husband, enjoying a glass of wine and a movie.

Website: www.rosiechapel.com

OTHER BOOKS BY ROSIE CHAPEL

Historical Fiction

The Hannah's Heirloom Sequence

The Pomegranate Tree - Book One

Echoes of Stone and Fire - Book Two

Embers of Destiny - Book Three

Etched in Starlight - Prequel

Hannah's Heirloom Trilogy - Compilation – e-book only

Prelude to Fate

Regency Romances

The Linen and Lace Series

Once Upon An Earl - Book One

To Unlock Her Heart - Book Two

Love on a Winter's Tide - Book Three

A Love Unquenchable - Book Four

A Hidden Rose - Book Five

The Daffodil Garden

The Unconventional Duchess

His Fiery Hoyden

A Regency Duet

A Regency Christmas Double

Fate is Curious

A Christmas Prayer *with Ashlee Shades*

The Pomegranate Tree

Hannah's Heirloom - Book One

Hoping to trace the origins of an ancient ruby clasp, a gift from her long dead grandmother, Hannah Wilson travels to the fortress of Masada with her best friend, Max. Strange dreams concerning a rebel ambush begin to haunt Hannah and following a tragic accident, she slips into the world of Ancient Masada.

A woman out of time, Hannah must rely on her instincts and her knowledge of what will befall this citadel to survive. Will she escape, or is she doomed to die along with hundreds of others as Masada falls – and what does any of this have to do with an ancient ruby clasp?

Echoes of Stone and Fire

Hannah's Heirloom - Book Two

Pompeii - a vibrant city lost in time following the AD79 eruption of Vesuvius. Now rediscovered, archaeologists yearn for an opportunity to uncover the town's past. Some things, however, are best left alone - revealing the secrets hidden beneath the stones could prove perilous. Hannah and Max are brought to Pompeii by a surprise invitation to join an excavation team who are trying to uncover the city's long history.

After entering an excavated house that bears a Hebrew inscription, Hannah's two worlds collide, and she falls back through time to ancient Pompeii. A place where her ancestor is a physician to gladiators engaged in mortal combat, where riotous mobs run amok and where a ghost from the past returns to haunt her.

Will Hannah and her loved ones manage to escape the devastation she knows is coming, before the town is engulfed in volcanic ash?

Will she ever find her way back to Max the love of her life, waiting not so patiently millennia away? Or will echoes be all that remain?

Embers of Destiny

Hannah's Heirloom - Book Three

AD80 - Hannah and Maxentius must embark on a new journey to Northern Britannia. This harsh frontier is far from the comforts of Rome and danger lurks where least expected; a garrison of soldiers, some unhappy with their isolated posting; local tribes, outwardly accepting of their Roman occupier, but who may still resent the seizure of their lands.

Millennia away, Hannah Vallier finds a familiar item while working in a museum near Hadrian's Wall. It is the pomegranate; carved by Maxentius on Masada. Before Hannah can discuss it with Max, disaster strikes! Believing her husband has been killed, Hannah retreats into the past, her soul melding with that of her ancestor, but with little idea of what they could face. Is the risk from the conquered tribes, or much closer to home?

As rebellion threatens to shatter a fragile peace, Hannah's heart whispers that just maybe Max isn't dead and that he is calling her home. Can she trust her heart, or will she remain caught out of time, her destiny floating away like embers on a breeze?

Etched in Starlight

Hannah's Heirloom - Prequel

Maxentius - a Roman soldier fresh from the battlefields of Armenia, arrives to take command of the military outpost of Masada, Herod's isolated citadel in the Judaean desert. A seemingly mundane posting after years of warfare, Maxentius finds it more challenging to maintain a focused garrison than to face the wrath of the Parthians across a disputed frontier.

Hannah - a young Hebrew physician spends her days dealing with injuries from street brawls, deprivation, disease and loss. As her beloved Jerusalem plunges into chaos; her brother — who belongs to a band of rebels determined to drive out their Roman occupiers — tells her of their plans to storm a desert fortress and steal the weapons stored there, persuading his reluctant sister to go with him.

Masada - following the ambush, Hannah finds and treats three badly wounded Roman soldiers. In the aftermath and against impossible odds, Hannah and Maxentius realise that they are more than healer and captive, their fate already etched in starlight.

꿈

Prelude to Fate

For Lucia, staring into the jaws of an horrific death, escape seems impossible.

Rufius Atellus, a veteran Roman soldier, is appalled when he recognises one of the victims about to be executed. Surely this is a ghastly mistake?

A ferocious she-wolf, anticipating a tasty meal, suddenly finds herself under a human's control.

In an unexpected twist, and as danger threatens, the lives of all three become inextricably entwined.

Was it chance brought them together in that theatre of bloodshed, or simply a prelude to fate?

꿈

REGENCY ROMANCE

Once Upon An Earl

Linen and Lace - Book One

When Fate saw fit to intervene in the life of Giles Trevallier, the very respectable Earl of Winchester, by dropping a female — soaked to the skin and with no memory of who she is or how she came to be there — literally at his feet, no one could have predicted the outcome.

While uncovering her identity, Giles realises he is falling hopelessly in love with his mystery guest, who unbeknownst to him, is succumbing to similar emotions; but, when the heart is involved, a thoughtless word or gesture can thwart even Fate's best-laid plans.

Faced with misunderstandings, whispers of scandal, secret documents and foreign agents, their chance at a happy ever after seems elusive, but fairy tales often happen when least expected, and love — however inconvenient — usually finds a way to conquer all.

To Unlock Her Heart

Linen and Lace - Book Two

Abused by a duke, and shunned by Society, relief seems at hand when Grace Aldeburgh is bequeathed a house in a small village, far from malicious gossips.

Once there, a tentative friendship blooms between Grace and Theo Elliott, the local doctor, who has already resolved to be the man to unlock her heart.

Just when happiness appears to be within her grasp, her erstwhile tormentor once again stalks Grace. After a failed kidnap attempt, the duke's quest culminates in an acrimonious confrontation, and the reason for his venal pursuit becomes agonisingly clear.

Love on a Winter's Tide

Linen and Lace - Book Three

Every day, Helena disappears into a world few acknowledge, helping the poor, downtrodden, and abused. A husband is the last thing she can be bothered with.

Busy managing his shipping line, Hugh Drummond sees no need for a wife, whose only joy is dancing and frivolity. If — and it was a huge if — he ever married, it would be to a woman as capable as he, not some giddy society Miss.

Then, Hugh meets Helena and despite their resolve, fate, it seems, has other ideas. As their attraction deepens however, treachery threatens to tear them apart. Will they uncover the perpetrator in time, or will their love be swept away, lost forever on a winter's tide?

A Love Unquenchable

Linen and Lace - Book Four

Jessica Drummond, a bright and cheerful young woman, rarely gives romance, let alone love, a thought. Long hours working in her brother's shipping office affords little chance of her ever meeting an eligible bachelor.

Duncan Barrington, veteran of the Napoleonic Wars, believes himself wounded in both body and soul. He has no intention of inflicting his demons on anyone, certainly not a beautiful and, in his opinion, irresponsible city lady.

One cold and snowy morning, the plight of a bedraggled puppy throws Jessica and Duncan together and, as a spark of something indefinable yet wholly unquenchable begins to burn, it is unclear who rescued whom.

A Hidden Rose

Linen and Lace - Book Five

After witnessing his mother's grief at the loss of his father, Nick Drummond resolved never to cause someone he loved such distress. Even the happiness of his siblings would not sway him – until he met Rose.

Rose Archer was almost content assisting her doctor father in a tiny fishing village in the north of Yorkshire. To experience the world beyond, a tantalising dream – until she met Nick.

Unexpectedly, the impossible becomes possible, and the renounced – desired above all things, but the shipwreck that brought them together, may yet tear them apart. Will Nick learn to trust his heart, or will his love for Rose remain forever hidden

The Daffodil Garden

Horrifically scarred during the war, William Harcourt - Marquis of Blackthorne - prefers to spend his days in the quiet of his daffodil garden; plants do not pity, turn away, or judge.

Lucy Truscott, whose life is far removed from that of the *ton*, has no idea that by saving the life of a young woman, to whom she bears an uncanny resemblance, her own will be placed in mortal danger.

A chance encounter leads to something more. William begins to trust that Lucy sees the man beneath the scars, while Lucy is persuaded that love might actually transcend status.

Unfortunately, before their courtship has really begun, someone has every intention of ending it - permanently.

The Unconventional Duchess

Refusing to suffer the humiliation of her husband flaunting his mistress at Society events, the newly married Duchess of

Wallingstead, Ella Lennox, takes control of her life. She leaves London for the family's country seat in remote Yorkshire.

A woman alone, Ella spends the next four years turning a cold, grim house into a home, and transforming the fortunes of the estate. Not afraid of hard work, she soon earns the respect of those around her with her determination and unconventional attitude.

Out of the blue, the duke arrives. Resigned to another arduous visit, Ella is stunned when it seems he is attempting to court her.

Impossible!

Could her dream of a happy marriage be about to come true?

Everything hangs on a snowstorm, a herd of cows and an uninvited guest!

His Fiery Hoyden

A Novella

Livvy has no respect for the nobility; they let her down when she most needed them. Why should she accede to their demands now?

Philip, Lord Harrington, is stunned to discover the young heir to the dukedom lives a stone's throw away in a ramshackle cottage, and resolves to restore the child to his birthright.

They meet in a clash of wills, but just when it seems Livvy might surrender, the victory Philip desires, may not taste all that sweet.

A Regency Duet

Luck be a Pirate

Luck wasn't something retired pirate Kennet Alexson believed in – good or bad. However, even he had to concede that landing a job at

Trentams shipyard, and meeting Lynette Collins, was more than coincidence.

Fortune it seemed, was smiling on him for once.

As Kennet adjusts to life on dry land, his friendship with Lynette deepens into something far more enduring, and what once seemed elusive now becomes possible.

Unfortunately, fate has other plans, and Kennet's good luck is about to run out.

The Highwayman's Kiss

Surrendered Hearts – Book One

Nothing exciting had ever happened to Juliette St Clair. Her days were spent assisting her father or calling on friends, wandering art galleries, taking constitutionals or, and more preferably, escaping into her books. Her evenings her evenings — an endless round of balls, where she preferred to remain invisible.

Until the day she was robbed by a highwayman.

A Regency Christmas Double

Heart Rescued

Four years since Jasper lost the woman he was hoping to marry. Four years since he closed his heart and withdrew from Society. He has no idea his reclusive existence is about to be shattered.

Enter his sister's best friend, Harriet, a flame haired beauty, who needs his help.

Reluctantly he agrees and as they spend time together, it is clear their feelings run deep. Although Harriet affects Jasper in a way no woman ever has, he believes her to be out of his league ~ but it's Christmas and she might just be the one to melt his frozen heart

Catch a Snowflake

Romance often blossoms in the most unlikely of places - but in a ward full of wounded soldiers - surely not?

When Lucas Withers comes face to face with Jemima Parsons - a young woman who blames him for her brother's injury - falling in love is the last thing on their minds. What neither of them anticipated, was the magic of snowflakes.

Fate is Curious

A Novella

Happily, ever after? No such thing! Bereft, following her beloved husband's sudden death, Lady Charlotte Sherbrooke has lost her belief in such romantic nonsense.

Successful shipping merchant, Zacharie Romain, is no stranger to loss; his business can be hazardous. Moreover, his wife died in childbirth and even though it happened a decade ago, he has no mind to expose himself to such sorrow again.

They meet in less than joyful circumstances but, as the year turns and grief diminishes, the woes of a small boy become the catalyst for something wholly unexpected. Can Charlotte and Zacharie trust what Fate has in store or will past heartbreak prevent them from taking a chance on love?

A Christmas Prayer

with Ashlee Shades

A Short Story

An entreaty from a frightened child.

Orphaned and only nine, Caroline Thorne has to grow up before her time. She is doing everything she can to keep what is left of her family together and out of the workhouse but is terrified her prayers are not being heard. Or maybe they are…

A petition from a woman desperate for a family.

A chance meeting with three orphaned siblings, tugs at Elizabeth Barrington's heart strings. Thus far, she and her husband have not been blessed with children and, as Christmas approaches, a plan begins to form - one which might just be the answer to her prayers.

Two Christmas prayers, as different as they are the same.

Will they hear and, more importantly, heed the answer?

The Lady's Wager

Surrendered Hearts- Book Two

A Novelette

Ged Mowbray will do anything to avoid being married off to the suitable prospects his parents insist on parading in front of him.

Melissa Bouchard is under no illusion her sizeable dowry is the attraction to suitors, not her.

An overheard conversation leads to an offer too good to refuse, but what happens when a lady's wager, becomes a gamble on the happily ever after, you did not even realise you wanted?

Winning Emma

Surrendered Hearts - Book Three

A Novelette

Randolph Craythorpe — earl, covert operative, and occasional highwayman — believed his dalliance with Lady Felicity Hartwich would lead to marriage. It did, but not to him! The arrival of an unwelcome guest, however, provides the perfect opportunity to indulge in a little retaliation.

Emma Newbury accompanies her cousin, Lady Charity Anscombe, to London for the Christmas season. Once there, she comes face to face with the three men who witnessed the humiliating aftermath of her father's disgrace — one of whom, to her irritation, has taken up residence in her dreams.

Their infrequent encounters only serve to confuse but, while winter tightens its grip on the city, what was inconceivable becomes the one thing for which they both yearn, yet bound by Society's rules, cannot admit.

As the snow falls, Randolph begins to understand that to win Emma, he will have to surrender.

FAIRY TALE ROMANCE

Chasing Bluebells

A Novella

Once upon a time, somewhere in France, there was a man whose reckless obsession led him down a dark path. One which, ultimately, cost him his life.

That ought to have been the end of it. Regrettably, as is so often the case, those who least deserve it, suffer for the actions of others.

A decade after being sent away, Sebastien Daviau returns to the little village where everything began, hoping to lay the ghosts of his childhood to rest, studiously ignoring the possibility, he might run into Charlotte de Montbeliard.

As luck would have it, Charlotte is the one who runs into him… well his horse. Although the encounter leaves a lasting impression, neither recognises the other.

A name revealed causes a freak accident, catapulting Sebastien's past into his present, and bringing him face to face with a man whose reputation would intimidate the most ardent of suitors.

Can whatever is blossoming between Charlotte and Sebastien survive the challenge imposed, or is their happily ever after about to fade as quickly as the bluebells they loved to chase?

§

CONTEMPORARY ROMANCE

Of Ruins and Romance

Kassandra Winters has intrigued Gabriel St Germain since he accidentally knocked her flying outside her university professor's office. Her face haunts his dreams, yet he never expected to see her again. So, he is surprised when she appears, as though destined to do so, in the middle of a ruin, and he concocts a plan to win her heart.

Gabriel's old-fashioned courtship touches something deep inside Kassie and, although struggling to believe someone as handsome as Gabriel could possibly be interested in her, she soon realises she has fallen irrevocably in love with him. However, just as Kassie shares everything of herself with Gabriel, her world comes crashing down.

Can their romance survive or will it fall in ruins, like the relics of antiquity that brought them together.

❧

All At Once It's You

When Alex arrives in the small village of Rosedale Abbey, to take up a position as a research assistant for a renowned archaeologist, the last thing she is looking for, or expects to find, is love.

Jake was perfectly happy with the status quo. When it came to relationships, he didn't do committed or long term. He called the shots, and if his current flame didn't like it, she knew what to do. A philosophy, which served him well - until he met Alex.

Romance blooms, but even as the untamed wilderness of the North Yorkshire moors weaves its spell, a long-buried secret might yet jeopardise their happily ever after.

§

Cobweb Dreams
A Novella

A holiday on the Scottish isle of Mull was just the break Chloe Shepherd needed, an escape from her boring office job and her complete lack of anything resembling a social life. Romance, it seems, isn't on the cards and, although Chloe dreams of finding her soulmate she is beginning to believe love is like cobwebs — spun overnight, only to vanish in the early morning breeze.

Under sufferance, Dominic Winters makes a flying visit to Mull to check on a rental property owned by his family. He hasn't got time for this — so indulging in a holiday fling is the last thing on his mind.

A lamb stuck in a bog proves a most unexpected matchmaker and, while Mull weaves its magic, Chloe wonders whether those fragile cobwebs might be far more stubborn than she thought.

§&

Just One Step
A Short Story

In the aftermath of an horrific car accident, Daisy Forrester travels to Italy - hoping, so far from her memories, she might begin to heal.

Archaeologist, and single father, Adam Willoughby is too busy looking after his young daughter to give romance let alone love, a thought.

Neither expects a chance encounter in an ancient ruin to be anything more, but sometimes, that's all it takes.

§&

His Heart's Second Sigh
A Novella

Reuben Faulkner and Paige Latimer are two happily single people, who have no desire to upset the status quo.

Unexpectedly, they are thrown together, only to discover both want far more than a casual friendship.

Just when things take an interesting turn, Reuben's past catches up with them, and threatens to derail their blossoming romance before it has chance to start.

§&